Fashionistas

THE INTERNS NOVELS
by Chloe Walsh

Book One: *Fashionistas*
Book Two: *Truth or Fashion*

Chloe Walsh

the INTERNS

Fashionistas

HARPER TEEN

An Imprint of HarperCollins*Publishers*

Typography by Amy Ryan

❖

First Edition

Fashionistas

"Fashion fades; only style remains the same."

Filed under: Fashionista > Style

Do you know who said that? Care to guess what it means? Well, my fellow <u>fashionistas</u>, allow me to enlighten you. It was that ultimate fashion icon, <u>Coco Chanel</u>. And what Coco was so classily saying is that you can buy all the $1,500 <u>Prada</u> handbags and $500 <u>Jimmy Choo</u>s in the world— you might even look pretty enough, dripping in all that high-end artillery—but, darling, if you don't have style, you simply don't have style.

I'd like to tell that to all the slavish fashion victims prancing down Madison Avenue who've shamelessly copied their outfits off the mannequins at <u>Barneys</u> with nary a thought— and the Fashionista doesn't like to name names, but I'm thinking of a certain Upper East Side » prep-school princess who recently dropped $3,500 on an exercise outfit, even though the girl hasn't worked out a day in her life. People, there's more to fashion than being able to buy it. You've got to work it. Work it in a glamorous <u>vintage flapper gown</u> purchased at your local thrift store OR in some extravagant piece straight from the latest <u>prêt-à-porter collections</u>. Just know your style, own your look, and be true to your most fabulous self.

It seemed fitting to open my premiere blog with a nod to Coco Chanel—even though Coco was long gone before blogs ever arrived on the scene. Fashion, after all, is about reinvention, taking something old and making it new again, taking a dress created by someone else, sliding it on, and making it look like it was made for you and only you.

Of course, to do that, you need style. And that's what I'm here for. More to come.

Your faithful Fashionista

1

Barneys or Bargain Basement?

"OH, DAMN."

Aynsley Rothwell glanced at her vintage lizard-skin Cartier Tank watch and threw a twenty at the cab driver. She paused in front of the gleaming glass towers of Conrad Publishing and checked her watch. It read eleven o'clock, same as it had when she came clattering out of her town house at least twenty-five traffic-jammed minutes ago. She'd warned the cabbie not to take Park Avenue. She pulled her BlackBerry Pearl out of her metal mesh tote bag. Noon. She was more than half an hour late for the first day of her summer internship at *Couture* magazine. Oh well. Aynsley knew that half an hour late in New York City time was positively prompt. And in the fashion industry, thirty minutes tardy was the gauche side of early.

She breezed past security and caught an elevator, all the while tapping at her watch. It had probably been broken for years. Not that Aynsley would've noticed. It's not like she ever wore the thing as a timepiece. She'd found it in Paris at the Saint-Ouen flea market two Christmases ago and had begged her dad for the 1,200 euros to purchase it. She never thought to make sure the thing actually worked.

Aynsley rode the elevator to the thirty-third floor with a blond Amazon whose cheekbones could have cut diamonds. The Glamazon gave Aynsley the once-over. She obviously coveted Aynsley's bag—by Eamon Sinds, a bad-boy Londoner who the Glamazon would discover along with the rest of America when his first stateside collection arrived in the fall. But she was also trying to see if Aynsley was carrying a portfolio. No doubt to figure out which modeling agency represented her. Click? Elite? Flash?

None of the above. Aynsley's waiflike figure—five feet ten in flats, a boobless, hipless size two—and her sexy, slouchy, pantherlike stride would've made her a natural on the catwalk, but she was so *not* interested.

Modeling was a job, and jobs were, *yawn*, a bore.

The elevator opened and Aynsley found herself face-to-face with a life-size Angelina Jolie—her lips in all their puckered glory graced a blowup of the latest *Couture* cover. The receptionist jumped out of her seat and quickly ushered Aynsley down the hallway. They passed rolling racks full of Miu Miu dresses, Dolce jackets, and Celine boots before arriving at the entrance to a glass-enclosed conference room.

"Aynsley, it's divine to see you—and where did you get that trapeze dress? It's positively fab."

"Kiki," Aynsley said, kiss-kissing *Couture*'s Gucci-clad deputy editor, Kiki Benedict. "It's a Stella. I got it in London. Limited edition."

"Of course you did. And you scored a Sinds bag. Clever girl. You're late, by the way, but you haven't missed much. Isabel decided to tear up the houndstooth spread that everyone but Dieter always loathed, so she and Dieter are doing their brainstorm dance."

Isabel Dupre was *Couture*'s editor in chief, and one of the most famous fashion icons in the world—more well-known, perhaps, than any of the top designers and models who covered the pages of the magazine she'd run for the past fifteen years. Dieter Glück was her creative director, her sidekick—or as Aynsley's mother sometimes called him, "Isa's bitch."

"I was just going over the basics with your fellow interns, Aynsley. Of course, *you* already know the basics," Kiki continued. She turned to face three girls sitting around a glass-and-steel table, amid a clutter of lipstick-stained Starbucks cups, Poland Spring bottles, and an untouched tray of croissants and bagels. "Aynsley's practically family around here. Her mom and Isabel studied at the Sorbonne together."

Aynsley brushed away the swoop of coal-black bangs that hung over her left eye to get a better look at her cohorts. They were looking a tad dumbstruck, like those see-no-evil, hear-no-evil, speak-no-evil monkeys. They'd probably all worked their asses off to get this gig. An internship at *Couture* was a platinum-plated key to the fashion world. That's what Aynsley's mother had told her, anyway, before she announced that she'd pulled *beaucoup* strings to land her one of this summer's four coveted slots. Then she'd warned Aynsley that if she blew it, the glittering party that was her life would be as *over* as Juicy sweats.

"Hey, Aynsley. I'm Nadine Van Buren." Out of one of the chairs popped a sexy, mocha-skinned girl, with a slick black bob and eyebrows that arched to the north pole. Even in her vertigo-inducing metallic platforms,

Nadine came up to Aynsley's shoulder, but what she lacked in height she made up for in oomph. The girl had curves in all the places where Aynsley had angles, and her clingy Pucci wrap dress kept no secrets.

"Nadine's a Philly girl," Kiki explained. "Great art scene happening in Philadelphia right now. She's also the star editor of her school newspaper."

"*And* I'm a photographer. I'll be shooting covers here before the summer's out," Nadine said, grinning.

"Yeah, well, you'll be shooting my designs then," said a voice that was too squeaky to match the bravado behind it. The voice cleared its throat, before continuing in a steadier tone. "I'm Callie Ryan."

Callie extended her hand to Aynsley as if Aynsley, too, were a fashion icon, as if she were someone to suck up to. *Sigh*. Hadn't she just graduated from high school?

Aynsley turned her smirky smile on Callie and saw that the girl's hazel eyes were boring into her like a laser. The look and the voice, they scratched something inside Aynsley, like fingernails down a chalkboard. She gave Callie an icier version of the up-down that the Glamazon in the elevator had given her. She had to admit, the squeaker was cute. Long, perfectly messy brown hair, bee-stung lips, legs that seemed to go all the way up to her boobs. Her outfit needed some help, though: She wore a lacy cami and a micromini made from a patchwork of crushed silk, faded denim, and black lace. The skirt was cut high enough to require a precautionary bikini wax, and the whole ensemble was a little too Hot Topic for the halls of *Couture*. Moving down Callie's legs, Aynsley stopped on her shoes. Strappy copper Sigerson Morrison sandals. So two seasons ago.

"I guess that means I'll be taking coffee orders," laughed the third girl. "I'm Ava Barton." Ava was pretty, but definitely the plainest of the lot, with straight brown hair and brown eyes. She had on a sailor-striped Armani Exchange sundress with a navy cardigan, an outfit that looked familiar. It was the exact ensemble Aynsley had seen on bus-shelter ads all spring.

"And I can definitely handle coffee," Ava continued. "I've got a close personal relationship with Starbucks." She smiled, showing off the kind of dimples not even the hottest Park Avenue surgeon could carve.

"Well, I take a triple cappuccino," Nadine said with an imperious wave of her hand. "Especially first thing in the morning, if you know what I mean."

"Triple cap, got it."

"My God, Ava, with that kind of ambition, you'll have Isabel's job in no time," Kiki said sarcastically. She gave Aynsley an almost imperceptible eye roll, which Aynsley pretended not to see.

"Who will have my job?" trilled a throaty French-accented voice. The conference room double doors flew open and in strode Isabel Dupre, a vision in a skin-tight white Gaultier summer suit that made her trademark spiky jet-black hair all the more striking. "Whomever it is, her first order of business should be sending Dieter back to Bavaria. *Houndstooth?* What was I thinking? I didn't like it in the eighties, and these things do *not* improve with time."

Isabel turned her violet-colored eyes on the interns. Though she was smiling, Aynsley felt a familiar lurch in her stomach. Isabel was one of the few people who shook Aynsley's nerves. Maybe it was because she was the High Priestess of Fashion. Maybe it was because Aynsley knew, from her mother's gossip, that the proverbial lash of Isabel's tongue could leave a girl bleeding. Or maybe it was because Isabel had the world's sharpest bullshit detector, and even if she didn't officially know that Aynsley had been forced to take this internship or else spend the summer in the upscale, Italian version of solitary confinement, she somehow *knew it* anyway.

"*Chère*," she said, kissing Aynsley's cheeks twice, Continental style, "I just spoke to your *maman*. I'm stopping over with them after I leave Donatella's yacht. How good of you to join us here instead of there."

There being the Rothwells' stone villa in Umbria. A villa that was miles away from the nearest village, that didn't even have a television, and whose pool was like one degree above freezing. It was surely the most boring place on earth, yet her parents loved it. Dad could manage the hedge fund by day and drink $500 bottles of wine by night. Aynsley's mother insisted she needed the two months of total quiet to "recharge" for her busy life on the charity-board circuit. Aynsley and her brother, Julian, wondered why their parents couldn't go to East Hampton or Saint-Tropez or Capri or any of the other places where their set summered.

"I am impressed that all of you are here." Isabel beamed out her eighteen-karat smile. "You worked hard for this internship, I know, but now is the time to work one hundred times harder. You must show us whether you are meant for Barneys or the bargain basement. But I don't need to tell you this obvious thing, do I, Callie, Ava, Nadine, Aynsley?"

A chorus of *no*s echoed throughout the room, along with one *no, ma'am* that made Aynsley wince. Isabel smiled secretively and continued. "*Très bien*. You girls beat out more than one thousand applicants. Now the only competition you have is each other, *non*?" Isabel laughed. "Just a joke. We're all friends here. *Bonne chance*," she called, and was out the door, leaving a cloud of Chanel behind her.

2

The Poor Girl's Marc Jacobs

CALLIE RYAN LIMPED along 42nd Street, her heels erupting with angry, wet blisters. When she won the auction on eBay for the strappy sandals that were now strangling her feet, she'd taken it as a sign. After all, hadn't she coveted these very shoes when she saw them in *Couture* a few years back at their original $325 price? There wasn't anywhere chic enough to wear Sigerson Morrison in Columbus, Ohio. But in New York? At *Couture*?

When Callie found out she had been selected for the internship, her first response was a round of screaming yelps that sent Chip, the family dog, scurrying under the table. Her second response was panic. What was she going to wear? Sure, she had her own Callie Ryan pieces. She'd been sewing since she was three, and half her wardrobe was of her own creation. But while she was eager to strut her own stuff, she knew that to compete with the starlets and socialites she read about constantly in *Us* weekly, she'd need some bonafide designer duds to go with her original pieces.

She combed eBay but hadn't found much she could afford, except for a few Betsey Johnson dresses, and the sandals—a steal at $35 (or so she thought, until she realized how unbearably uncomfortable they were). DailyCandy had said that Forever 21 was the "poor girl's Marc Jacobs," so Callie also charged up a ton of their skirts, dresses, camis, and blouses online. To be on the safe side, though, she'd cut out all the Forever 21 labels before she packed her bags for Manhattan. If anyone asked, she'd say her new outfits were sample-sale finds.

"Are you okay?" Ava asked, slowing her pace for Callie to catch up.

Callie grimaced. "Yeah. Thanks. I guess I just didn't realize how much walking I'd be doing." She'd marched five blocks to the subway this morning, then she'd tromped through the mini office marathon that was the *Couture* orientation tour. She'd made her way to Personnel to fill out paperwork. She'd combed every inch of the shiver-inducing fashion closet, with its racks of Prada, Yves Saint Laurent, Calvin Klein, Valentino, and Versace. She'd even strolled through the drool-inducing beauty department, admiring a vast array of eye shadows, glosses, and lipsticks. By the time she'd made it to the building cafeteria (which had leather banquettes and space-aged light fixtures, not to mention sushi on the menu), Callie's feet were rebelling.

Ava laughed sympathetically. "Now you know why New Yorkers are so skinny. They walk everywhere. Don't worry, your feet will toughen up."

Callie smiled. Ava seemed real, like someone she might meet back in Columbus. Aynsley, on the other hand, seemed, well, like someone you'd meet in New York. Like someone you'd read about in *Women's Wear Daily*. Like the kind of person Callie hoped to be one day. Nadine was all attitude, with a less than classy style, at least judging by her weird wardrobe, half of which was currently strewn all over the New York University dorm room they'd been assigned to share for the summer.

"Where are we going?" Callie called to Aynsley and Nadine. When orientation ended, Aynsley had set off for the elevators, motioning for the other girls to follow her, and Nadine had been jogging ever since to keep pace with her leggy stride. After exiting the sparkling glass towers of the office building, Aynsley took off down 42nd Street. Callie had tried to stay in step with her—she was *dying* to know more about the socialite— but her sore feet wouldn't allow it. Now Aynsley and Nadine were almost half a block away, chatting like old pals and Callie felt a tinge of jealousy. She had to catch up. "Isn't the subway the other way?" she asked.

Just then Aynsley stopped, tossing her absurdly perfect hair—which was, of course, midnight black. (Aynsley was too cool for something as clichéd as bleach blonde.) She extended her slender arm into the air. A taxi crossed two lanes of traffic to stop in front of her. Nadine waved Ava and Callie over, then jumped into the cab alongside Aynsley. Callie jumped in next to her. Ava sat up front.

Now *this* was more like it, Callie thought. "Where are we going?" she asked, trying to sound blasé.

"I'm rescuing you from dorm food," Aynsley said with a mischievous smirk. "We can't have you gaining your freshman fifteen this summer."

"Not gonna happen to me," Nadine said. "I can eat and eat and eat, and it falls right off me."

"Looks like it goes straight to your booty," Aynsley said.

"If that were the case, I'd be eating day and night to boost my assets," Nadine shot back.

"Your assets . . ." Aynsley said, then paused, "seem pretty *boosted* already."

"That's right, girl. Admire the merchandise," Nadine replied, dragging her hand down her body like she was a spokesmodel selling Nadine Van Buren.

Callie observed this back-and-forth, looking for a way to insinuate herself into the conversation, but Nadine and Aynsley might as well have been talking in a foreign language that Callie understood but couldn't speak. She pressed her pert nose against the window, staring at the Hudson River glittering in the setting sun, and tried to think more positively. Here she was. Callie Ryan. Employee (sort of) at *Couture*. Zooming around New York City in a cab with Aynsley Rothwell. She'd made it here at last. Now she had to *really* make it here.

The cab turned off the highway onto a series of zigzagging cobblestone streets. This, Aynsley told them, was the Meatpacking District. "Used to be full of transvestite hookers," she said a little nostalgically. "But now it's *the* area. All the best restaurants and shopping are here. Jeffrey, Stella McCartney, Alexander McQueen, all on West 14th."

Callie made a mental note. She'd have to come back on the weekend to check it out, maybe see about getting the boutiques to stock a couple of her designs.

There was a line of people in front of the ultra-chic Palais restaurant, but Aynsley made her way past the rail-thin hipster couples and the leggy model wanna-bes to an unbelievably gorgeous black girl holding a clipboard—she was a ringer for Rihanna. Five minutes later Aynsley, Callie, Ava, and Nadine were seated at a big round table on the patio, just a Manolo's throw away from—

"Wow! Is that Sarah Jessica Parker?" Callie exclaimed.

"*Shhh,*" Aynsley scolded, looking embarrassed. Callie clamped her mouth shut, unsure of what sin she'd committed, but judging from Aynsley's disgusted expression, she guessed it wasn't cool to point at celebrities. Obviously, she had a lot to learn.

A bottle of champagne was delivered to the table and, just as Callie started to wonder how she was going to pay her share, Aynsley pulled out a black American Express card. "Dinner's on Gregory Rothwell," she said. She looked around and waved at some diners across the patio. "I can't believe how many people are still in the city. If I had a choice, I'd have made tracks out of here the minute I finished my last final."

"You just graduated high school, right?" Nadine asked.

"Thank God," Aynsley exclaimed. "One more day at Dalton and I'd simply die of boredom."

"Oh, you went to Dalton?" Ava asked her. "My freshman-year roommate at Vassar went there."

"What's her name?" Aynsley asked.

Callie saw Ava blush and stumble, but then Nadine jumped in.

"I was gonna apply to Vassar, but Poughkeepsie is much too small for *this* city girl. I'll be starting at Penn this fall."

"Impressive," Ava said with genuine admiration.

"Everyone wanted me. I got offers up the wazoo," Nadine said. "Washington U. Williams. Reed. Full ride at some. But *you know*. Ivy League—can't say no to that. Where are you going next year?" she asked Aynsley.

Aynsley swished the champagne around in her flute and sipped it. "I'm taking a gap year," she said.

"Like Prince William did," Callie blurted. Back when she was younger, she'd had a huge crush on the future king of England.

Aynsley just shrugged. There was something about her that was effortless and blasé. It made Callie hate her and want to be her all at once.

"What about you?" she asked, turning to Callie without actually looking at her. "You're still in high school, right?"

"Yep," Callie said, feeling proud that she was the youngest of the interns and happy that Aynsley had acknowledged her—sort of—at last. "I'll be a senior next year."

"Where do you go?" Aynsley asked her.

"Bexley Prep," she said, gulping champagne so fast that it stung her throat and made her eyes water. She was astonished by how easily the prep school lie had sprung up. There was no Bexley Prep. There was Bexley High School, a regular old public school, where she actually went. But the other girls didn't seem to notice. And the fib seemed to instantly put Callie on more equal footing with Aynsley.

"Boarding school?" Aynsley quizzed.

"Day school," Callie replied, feeling herself warm to the lie. Maybe it was the bubbly. "My father wanted me to go to Choate, but my mother wouldn't hear of sending me away, so they agreed on Bexley. It's a very small, very exclusive school in the Midwest."

"I think I've heard of it," Nadine said.

"Many have," Callie said in a posh voice as she refilled her flute.

The waiter came over to take their orders. Nadine asked for a cheeseburger with fontina; Ava, the salade Niçoise, dressing on the side. Aynsley ordered a "blood-rare" *steak frites*, which Callie noted was the most expensive thing on the menu, while Callie selected the penne puttanesca, which was at least a little familiar. She was pretty sure it was the one with the bacon.

"Another bottle of Bollinger?" the waiter asked Aynsley.

"I think we'll switch to red. Let's have some of the Côtes du Rhône I had last week."

"Good choice," he said with a smile.

"Wow!" Callie exclaimed after the server had retreated. "Even the waiters here look like models."

"Wow?" Aynsley asked with a smirk. "Bexley girls are easily impressed, huh?"

Callie felt her ears go red as she realized she'd messed up again. She was going to have to be more careful.

While they waited for their food to arrive, the girls talked about themselves. Ava was from Long Island, planned on getting a degree in journalism, and loved fashion. Nadine had won a national journalism contest for an article and photo essay about some homeless artists who opened a gallery in Philly, and she'd had two pieces published in *Seventeen*. Callie told the girls about wanting to be a designer since she was a kid, and told them about her latest obsession, handbags and accessories. She sort of bragged that she'd sold a couple of her purses in one of Columbus's most exclusive boutiques, which, as she rationalized, was almost true. She *had* sold a couple of her pieces at a community swap meet, and in the fashion desert that was Ohio, surely that qualified as a hip shop.

Aynsley kept jumping up from the table to chat with her friends—it seemed like she knew half the restaurant—but in between her tête-à-têtes, Callie learned that Aynsley did not design clothes and knew nothing of journalism. She hinted that she'd gotten the internship because of her mother's relationship with Isabel Dupre, which instantly made Callie feel superior. But as the conversation went on, and the girls talked designers, any momentary feelings of superiority faded. The thing with Aynsley was, even if her internship was an act of nepotism, it still seemed like she knew more than the rest of them combined. It wasn't just that her designer clothes were *this* season. It wasn't just that she could get past the velvet rope at Tenjune whenever she pleased. It wasn't even that she had a black American Express card tucked into her Chanel wallet nestled in her Eamon Sinds bag. Even in Levi's and a plain tee, Aynsley would radiate that *thing*. Callie didn't even know the word for it, wasn't sure what *it* was exactly, but she knew that she wanted more of it. In between picking at her pasta—it wasn't the one with bacon, it was the one with anchovies—she studied Aynsley.

Aynsley's BlackBerry had been ringing all night. Every time she'd peer at the caller ID and let the call go to voice mail, as if she were just too busy to be so popular. But as they were finishing up their meals, Aynsley got a call she deemed worth answering.

"You're late," she snapped. Pause. "I said Palais. Not Stanton Social." Pause. "Just cab over here." Pause. "We're on the patio. Colette's hostessing. She'll send you over. Who're you with?" Pause. "Please lose Walker. He's such a bore." Pause. "Okay. See you soon."

"Please don't tell me that's Walker *Graystone* you're brushing off," Nadine said, waving the waiter over for another bottle of wine.

Callie perked up. Walker Graystone was the city's

latest It Boy, party promoter, sometimes fashion model, video director—all at the age of twenty-four. Aynsley *knew* him?

"More like *Stalker* Graystone," Aynsley replied. "We went on *one* date. He took me to some dive Mexican place with a secret back room just because he'd seen Jay-Z there. Then he got wasted and tried to make out with me. Slobberville. I was so not interested. And, naturally, now that I don't want to see him again, he's all in love. He's pestering me to be in the latest video he's directing," she added. "And he's glommed onto my brother, Julian, who's on his way over here—*sans* Walker, let's hope."

"Guys are so predictable that way," Nadine said. "I hooked up with this total player at my school. All the girls were drooling over him. We had one night together and, you know, my itch was scratched—I was ready to move on. But he'd had a taste of me, and he wanted himself another slice. He started writing me love letters. Poems. Wanting to go to the prom. It was a riot."

"Play them or they'll play you," Callie said in the knowing tone of the girl she wished she was. She'd had a few boyfriends, though nothing serious. But she'd practically memorized that old dating book *The Rules*, and now she felt like she was better equipped to handle New York's infamous crop of hot bachelors.

"Do guys get better in college?" Nadine asked Ava. "You know, in every which way?"

Ava blushed, then shrugged. "I wouldn't really know."

"Vassar's not all-girls still, is it?" Aynsley asked.

"No, there's guys. I just don't have a lot of experience with them."

"Don't tell me you've never had a boyfriend?" Nadine asked.

"Not really," Ava said quietly.

"A hook-up?" Callie asked.

Ava shook her head and smiled, looking embarrassed but sweet.

"You're a . . ." Nadine began.

"Yes," Ava said firmly. "Can we please move on?" She looked genuinely pained.

"No, we cannot move on. Not until we take care of business," Nadine said. "Ladies. We have ourselves a project."

"Maybe I'll send Walker your way," Aynsley offered. "Oh, here's Jules." She jumped up and waved.

As Julian Rothwell strode through the restaurant, all the patrons—male, female, gay, straight—watched him. At six feet tall, he had the same lanky build and dark hair as his sister, but his five-o'clock shadow gave his pretty face a faintly dangerous, definitely sexy look. Still, it was the eyes that got you: gray-blue-green, with a wicked, amused expression, like he'd just been to the hottest party *and* had the hottest sex, and *no*, he wasn't going to tell you about either of them.

All night long Callie had been counting the ways in which Aynsley's life was charmed, but here was an area where Callie was ahead. At least she wasn't related to a biscuit like Julian. Meaning she could date a biscuit like Julian if she played her cards right.

Julian waltzed through the restaurant, two impossibly skinny blondes trailing behind him. "Sly, baby," he called, planting a kiss on his sister's cheek. "How's the working world?" he asked, laughing.

"Screw you, Jules," Aynsley replied affectionately. "Hi Elena. Hey Marina."

"Hi," intoned the gorgeous blondes.

"Sly's got a gig at *Couture*," Julian told his pretty companions, his eyes dancing mischievously. "And she has to be a good girl, working forty-hour weeks, or else."

"Or else what?" Nadine asked.

"*Il prigione,*" Julian said.

"English," Nadine demanded.

"He said 'prison.' Which is a tad dramatic. My parents gave me the choice between the internship or the summer in Italy."

"Poor baby," Callie said sarcastically, finding it hard to feel sorry for Aynsley. She'd never even *been* to Italy.

Aynsley's dark eyes flashed. "Milan or Rome or Florence would be great—all the restaurants, clubs, boutiques, ateliers. But my parents' place is in the middle of nowhere."

Callie felt foolish, like she should have known the various echelons of Italian chicness, but then Julian smiled at her.

"Sly barely passed Italian," Julian explained. "So she'd be stuck with a tutor all summer."

"I know enough Italian. *Va fanculo*, for instance," Aynsley demonstrated.

"Now, now," Julian said. "No need for profanity. And you should see Sly's teacher," he continued, turning his gaze on Callie. "Some fifty-year-old letch. When I had an Italian tutor, she was hot, and she taught me a whole different kind of conjugation. But Gregory and Cecilia can't even get Aynsley a proper boy toy to play with," Julian said, patting his sister's head. "So poor Sly had to join the working masses."

"I'd hardly call *Couture* the working masses," Callie said, widening her eyes and cocking her head to the side so her hair brushed over her bare shoulder. "I mean, Aynsley gets to spend the whole day with us, for instance."

"Mitigating factors, for sure," Julian said. "Sly, you going to introduce me to your colleagues?"

"This is Ava Barton and Nadine Van Buren," Aynsley said, acknowledging both girls with a nod.

"Philly's finest," Nadine said, shoving out her ample chest for Julian to see. He smiled vaguely, like he was used to having boobs shoved in his face.

Aynsley continued. "And this is Callie—what's your last name?"

"Ryan."

"Luck of the Irish?" Julian asked playfully.

"My dad's side. Yes," Callie said with a smile.

"The freckles give you away, if not the name."

For the first time in her life, Callie was grateful for the little smattering of dots over the bridge of her nose.

"Callie's in high school," Aynsley interjected. "Julian heads back to Brown in the fall."

"Which makes me the golden child, and Little Miss Aimless over here, the prodigal daughter," Julian explained. "That's why she's working all summer. And

I'm off to the Hamptons tomorrow. You girls should come up for the weekend—the work week does still end on Friday, doesn't it?"

"I'd love to go to the beach," Callie said. "I could use some sun." She rubbed her long legs, glad that she'd just waxed them. Out of the corner of her eye, she saw Julian admiring the view.

"Check, please," Aynsley called.

"Come on by," Julian offered. "Big party at Walker's."

"I'd rather eat glass," Aynsley replied. "We're staying in the city."

"What about Ava?" Callie asked. "You know? You could set her up."

Aynsley eyed Callie hard. "We'll find Ava someone more her speed."

"Shame," Julian said. He grabbed his sister's wineglass and drained it. "Speaking of Walker, we left him at Stanton Social, so I've got to motor. Care to join us?"

YES! Callie thought, hoping to tag along, but Aynsley flashed a bitchy smile and said, "Can't. Working girls and all. Got to be up early tomorrow. Catch that worm."

Julian gave a lopsided grin, winked, and was gone. Aynsley paid the check and glanced at her BlackBerry.

"It's barely ten," she said. "What do you say we go hit the poolside lounge at the Gentry?"

Callie suddenly felt tired, her champagne and wine buzz was fermenting into a headache. Keeping up the Callie Ryan prep-school-girl persona was exhausting and her feet were killing her. Besides, tomorrow was the first day of the rest of her life, and she wasn't about to blow it. Especially if a run-in with Julian wasn't in the cards. "I think I'll call it a night," she said.

"Me too," said Ava.

"Ohh, too bad," Aynsley said, sounding not all that disappointed. "What about you, Van Buren?"

"Lead the way, Sly," Nadine said.

Out on Ninth Avenue, Nadine and Aynsley flitted north to the glittering Gentry Hotel. Callie started to hobble in the vague direction of NYU, wondering if anyone walked barefoot in New York.

Ava smiled sympathetically. "How about we share a cab?" she suggested.

Callie nodded, and then, just as she'd seen Aynsley do, stuck out her arm—and for good measure, a leg—and a taxi screeched to a stop right in front of her.

3

It's not Hermès. It's Hermine.

NADINE WOKE UP the next morning with a drumbeat of a headache pounding in her temples and a mouth as dry as sandpaper. Damn, that had been one crazy night out. Aynsley might look like a wisp, but—pound for pound—the girl could party.

She looked at the clock. 8:45. Ugh. What time had they come home? Three o'clock? Four o'clock? Last night was already kind of a blur. Nadine remembered that after Aynsley had grown bored of the Gentry's rooftop bar—or, more likely, all the cloying Eurotrash guys and their artfully shaved stubble—she'd dragged Nadine to West Chelsea. It was a pretty desolate area, but incongruously set between a factory and an auto fix-it shop was a bar called Glass. Or was it Ice? Nadine couldn't remember. She did remember a black velvet rope and a line of people clamoring to get past the Prada-suited bouncer. Sly, of course, had cruised right in, leading Nadine into a cavernous room full of gleaming granite, polished concrete, and beautiful people. After Glass/Ice, things got a little hazy. Aynsley kept guiding them into cabs, which took them to similarly sleek bars full of fabulous party people. Nadine had a vague recollection of spotting a Hilton sister somewhere. One thing was for sure: Judging by her throbbing head, she'd had a few too many Ketel One martinis.

Nadine squinted in the morning light and peered around the room. Mrs. Rothwell clearly had a thing for flowers. The pink-and-peach wallpaper had a rose motif, the ornate brass bed's headboard was decorated with vines, and the shabby chic antique white armoire had little purple lilacs stenciled on it. The bedspread was floral print, as were the piles of throw pillows. "Mother's decorating motto is 'more is more,'" Nadine remembered Aynsley announcing the night before, after they'd stumbled out of a cab into the Rothwells' huge brownstone. "This is the least appalling of the guest rooms," she'd added, gesturing toward a doorway on the second floor. Then she'd handed Nadine a bottle of Evian and a pair of silk Calvin Klein pajamas and disappeared.

Nadine padded out of bed and into the hallway. "Sly?" she called quietly. "*Sly?*" she repeated a little louder. No answer. She followed the mahogany staircase downstairs to the foyer. She looked in the parlor, the enormous chef's kitchen, the perfectly manicured back garden, but there were no signs of life, save for a mop bucket next to a small wooden back staircase. Nadine headed back upstairs, counting, then losing count of all the rooms: bedrooms, libraries, dens, TV rooms, parlors, at least six bathrooms. Everything was decorated in the same overwrought style. It was like Mrs. Rothwell had digested and then regurgitated a collection of *Victoria* magazines.

At the end of the hallway on the third floor was a closed door. Nadine rapped on it lightly. No one answered, but the door edged open. Aynsley's room was as minimalist as the rest of the house was maximalist. White walls, and a low Japanese platform bed with matching tables. The black lacquered floor exposed wall-to-wall, except for a funky cream-colored shag rug. A plasma TV on one wall, and a Bose sound system with a custom-designed ruby-encrusted iPod docked into it. With the exception of the plasma and three huge black-and-white Richard Avedon photos, the walls were completely bare. Aynsley was passed out in the middle of the bed, her ebony hair spilling out on the taupe sheets.

"Rise and shine, Sly," Nadine called. "We've got places to go, people to meet."

Aynsley groaned, waved Nadine in the general direction of the bathroom, pulled the pillow over her head, and rolled back over. Nadine loped toward the bathroom but was stopped in her tracks by the siren's call of Aynsley's closet. It was the size of Nadine's dorm room and had obviously been specially designed to fit Sly's humongous wardrobe. Everything was perfectly categorized: long skirts, short skirts, microminis; casual dresses, dressy dresses, evening gowns; Dolce jeans, Sevens, Paul & Joes; jackets, sweaters (all cashmere) in a rainbow of colors; trench coats, leather jackets, wool wraps. And then there was the mother lode: three ten-foot-long racks full of shoes. Nadine grabbed a patent leather Gucci stiletto and turned it over. "Looks like Miss Thang's a size seven. Now that's lucky, 'cause so am I." Nadine spied a pair of Manolo slides the color of a bruise. "Come here, my pretties," she murmured, slipping them on. "Now I've got to find something to go with you," she said. She rifled through the racks, settling on an electric purple Missoni crochet-knit dress with a periwinkle slip and ribbon trim. "You're gonna learn what it feels like to hug a real body," Nadine said to her reflection as she held the dress up before her.

She ran a hand across her head. Uh-oh. Her hair. It was a shoulder-length reddish-brown kinky mess, flattened down from bedhead and from wearing that black bob wig yesterday. What to do? With her pounding head, no way could she handle wearing the wig again, and her hats and falls were all down at the dorm. Hmm. She opened a mirrored door and found a series of drawers. Undies (lots of La Perla thongs), stockings (mostly fishnets), PJs (silk boxers and camis), and finally, scarves. She dug through the silky pile until she spied a purple and orange Asian print number. *Perfect*.

She jumped into the bathroom—all gray tile and marble and noveau Roman taps—and showered. Then she wrapped up in an ultraplush Frette towel and slathered herself liberally with Acqua di Parma moisturizer. She put on her new ensemble, tying the scarf around her head like a turban. She checked out her reflection in the mirror. Her glued-on lashes had survived the night. She threw on some bronzer and some

Mac Viva Glam courtesy of Aynsley's vanity drawer. When she was finished, she blew herself a kiss.

Aynsley was rousing as Nadine swirled out of the bathroom. When she spotted Nadine, her cat-shaped eyes widened. "You're wearing my clothes," Aynsley said wearily.

"They were getting lonely, so I liberated them," Nadine explained. "That's one hell of a collection you've got in there."

Aynsley pushed away the covers and sat up straight, but then the color drained out of her olive face and she lay back down. She groaned. Then hiccupped. "How are you so perky?" she asked weakly. "I cannot believe how much we drank. I think I'm still wasted."

"You look drunk," Nadine said, stepping closer to the bed. She sniffed. "And you smell drunk, too. You better get up and shower. We've got to be at *Couture* in forty minutes."

Aynsley pulled her hair away from her face and tied it into a bun. "Work. *Fabulous*," she said.

"Ahh, sarcasm," Nadine noted. "You must be rally-ing."

Aynsley gave Nadine the once-over. "That's supposed to be an A-line minidress, you know," she said gesturing to the purple Missoni, which on Nadine was transformed into a body-hugging, to-the-thigh number that was one inch away from being obscene. Nadine just smiled and ran her hands down her body, patting her booty, which was straining against the tight knit.

"And that turban thing?" Aynsley asked. "Is that my scarf?"

Nadine grinned. "Looks fabulous this way, doesn't it?"

"That's an Hermès scarf. Do you have any idea how much that costs?"

"Not the tiniest inkling," Nadine admitted. "But today, it's not Herm*ès*, it's Her*mine*."

"Fine, whatever," Aynsley said. "I'm going back to sleep."

"No, you're not," Nadine said, pulling off the duvet. "You're gonna show me how to work that fancy-ass espresso machine you got downstairs and then we're getting ourselves to work."

"Ask Marta to do it," Aynsley said. "She's lurking down there somewhere."

"Get up, girl. C'mon. You shouldn't party like you do if you can't handle the morning after."

Aynsley shot Nadine a lethal look, which Nadine repelled with a raised eyebrow. Sure, Aynsley was gorgeous, she had a wardrobe to rival *Couture*'s sample closet, and she obviously had more money than God, but Nadine planned to teach her that Philly girls don't scare easily. Aynsley seemed to get the message, because she relented. "Fine, Van Buren," she said with a sigh. "Let's go caffeinate."

"Atta girl. Nice crib you got, Sly," Nadine said as they walked down the stairs. "Very Zen."

"Thanks. I designed it myself. It's my sanctuary in Cecilia's gilt palace."

Aynsley made them both triple cappuccinos, and they sat side by side in the Rothwells' huge country kitchen. Nadine couldn't help but notice that the copper pots hanging from the ceiling looked like they'd never been used, and when she opened the hidden Sub-Zero, it was practically empty, save for Evian and Diet Cokes. She was starving. As Aynsley sipped her coffee and rubbed her head, Nadine nosed around in the pantry for something to eat. Truffles. Olives. Oyster crackers. Escargots. Where was the real food?

"Will you stop poking around?" Aynsley said. "You're making me nervous."

"I'm famished, Sly. Don't you people eat?"

"Yes, in restaurants. There's a Le Pain Quotidien on the corner, we can stop there—" Aynsley was interrupted by the phone. The electronic ringing seemed to physically pain her, judging by the way she winced. And when Cecilia Rothwell's voice clicked on, loud and clear from four thousand miles away, Aynsley grimaced in such obvious discomfort that Nadine felt a little sorry for the charmed girl.

"Aynsley darling, if you are hearing this, then you are already late for work. Which would make it the second day in a row. Not a particularly promising start, is it?" Nadine couldn't help but notice how Cecilia Rothwell's voice, though floaty and mellifluous, had an edge of steel to it. "I may be in Italy, but don't you doubt that I've got eyes all over the city. And this is your last chance, Aynsley. You blow it at *Couture* and you are on the first flight over here, and your father told me to add that you'll be flying coach." There was a self-satisfied chuckle. "If you're at work, good girl, but if, as I suspect, you're lying in bed screening, get that lazy *derrière* of yours in gear and get to *Couture*. Now. Or else you are beyond cut off. Ohh, time for my cooking class. Love you. *Ciao ciao*." And with that, Mrs. Rothwell hung up.

"Damn, your mom sounds even tougher than mine," Nadine said. "I thought your brother was kidding."

Nadine smiled at Aynsley, trying to commiserate,

but Aynsley wouldn't smile back. For a split second, her perfect veneer cracked, and Nadine could tell that she was either pissed or embarrassed or both. Then, just like that, it was as if a veil had descended over her face. "You'd better go," Aynsley said, doing her best imitation of a cold-hearted bitch.

"*You'd* better go," Nadine said. "Didn't you hear the message?"

"I heard it. And the message was meant for *me*. You could've given me some privacy. Don't you dare say anything."

"I don't know why you're flipping out," Nadine shot back. "Julian already told everyone about the Italy threat."

"Julian talks out his ass," Aynsley barked. "You worry about keeping your own mouth shut."

"Look, don't be aiming your fire at me," Nadine protested. "It's not my fault that your mom's being a bitch. And from what I saw at dinner last night," she added, "I'm not your new frenemy—but if I were you, I'd keep my eye out for little country Callie."

Aynsley's lips twitched into a sliver of a grin. Nadine could tell that the Ice Queen was starting to warm to her. "You're right," Aynsley said. "But I still have to shower, and it will be better if one of us arrives on time.

You cover for me, okay? Tell Kiki I stopped by the Coach showroom to get a peek at their fall designs. You'd better take a cab," she said, thrusting a twenty into Nadine's hand. "And tell the cabbie *not* to take Park Ave."

4

A Fancy, Frilly Frederick's of Hollywood

AVA BARTON STARED at her reflection in the mirror and sighed. Somehow, even with all the right accoutrements—a pea green Marc Jacobs silk ruched skirt, a matching green-and-white tank, and a pair of beaded Calypso sandals—Ava felt her look was, as always, *less* than the sum of its parts. Aynsley would look hipper than she would in a Glad bag, and Nadine had a super-funky style that Ava was pretty sure she herself could never pull off. As for Callie, not only did she look like she'd stepped out of the pages of a fashion magazine (okay, maybe not *Couture*—more like *Lucky* or *Style*), but her original designs were amazing. Ava had no doubt that one day Callie would be the toast of *Couture*. Ava, at least, could say she knew her when—maybe she'd even get to write her profile. One thing Ava *could* do was string together a decent sentence.

Ava turned her attention back to the mirror. She clasped her thick brown hair in her hands. Maybe an exotic hairdo would pull her outfit together. She piled her tresses atop her head, but it looked a mess. Next, she tried a sophisticated chignon at the nape of her neck, à la Gwyneth. That didn't look right either, so she twisted her hair into two thick braids, and it actually looked pretty cute. Ava smiled, her dimples reflecting back at her. Then she imagined her braided self at *Couture*, with the faces of Scarlett, Angelina, and Reese staring down at her, and she lost her nerve. In the end, she threw her hair into the same ponytail she wore every day, dusted her nose with Stila powder, and applied her favorite nude Prada lip gloss. She grabbed her pink Kate Spade peacock tote and took the stairs down two flights to Callie and Nadine's dorm room.

"Oh my god. I am so frigging excited," Callie burbled when Ava knocked on her door. "Here," she said, thrusting a Starbucks venti iced coffee at Ava. "You better catch up with me. I've already had two."

Ava accepted the coffee with a gracious smile. She

felt, for about the twenty-fifth time since orientation, amazed by her competition. From what she'd heard about *Couture*, she'd expected the other interns to be a bunch of entitled Upper East Side airheads whose idea of good journalism was *Us* weekly. Instead, she'd been paired with a pack of smart, ambitious, together girls, who seemed uniquely talented. Even Aynsley, who actually *was* an entitled Upper East Side girl, was about as much of an airhead as Isabel Dupre herself.

"You look adorable, by the way," Callie continued. "That color really brings out your eyes."

"Thanks," Ava said, finally taking in Callie's outfit. It was unlike anything she'd ever seen, while at the same time resembling something you'd expect to see on an Olsen twin. Her skirt was a jaggedly hemmed asymmetrical number, with triangular cutouts of silver netting material that looked like metal. It had a kind of punky, sultry, peek-a-boo look. Callie wore a halter top made of the same silver netting over a nude camisole. It scooped down to her waist, revealing perfectly square shoulders and a honey-tanned back. "You look amazing, Callie. Did you make that?"

Callie beamed, and her face flushed. "Everything but the shoes," she said, pointing to her silver wedges. "Aerosoles. Don't tell anyone. I had to buy them. My

feet are in shreds from yesterday. But I made the bag,"
she said, showing off a purple raw silk tote covered in a
collage of velvet patches.

"Amazing," Ava repeated.

"Wow. You really think so? God, I hope they notice
me. I really feel like this internship at *Couture* is my
golden ticket. Don't you?"

"Uh, yeah. Sure," Ava agreed. "We should go.
Where's Nadine?"

Callie's perky mouth shriveled in distaste, like she'd
just eaten a lemon. "*Nadine* never came home last
night. She probably glommed onto Aynsley and
weaseled herself into a sleepover. Did you see the way
she was kissing Aynsley's ass at Palais? It was beyond
embarrassing."

"I didn't really notice," Ava said shyly. "But I guess
we'll see them there, right?"

When Ava and Callie arrived at *Couture*, the receptionist sent them into a small windowless room where several boxes full of the July issue were waiting for them.
Just as they sat down to admire the issue, Nadine
arrived, her honey-colored skin looking a little peaked.
Two seconds later, Kiki strode in, wearing a black
Celine linen dress with a triple gold chain belt slung

over her nonexistent hips.

"You need to send copies of this issue out to all the photographers, designers, and writers who worked on it," Kiki began. "Here's a list of who did what, with addresses. Here are some sticky notes to flag the right pages, and then you attach this note from Isabel to the cover," she said, pointing to a thick stack of cream-colored note cards. Each one was embossed with *ID*, and hand-signed *Merci, Toujours, Isabel*. Ava noticed the cards smelled ever so faintly of gardenias. "I'll be back for you in an hour," Kiki continued, "and I expect these to be done."

"Where's Aynsley?" Callie asked.

"She had to stop by the Coach showroom, checking in on their fall designs," Nadine answered.

"Now, that, my dears, is the kind of initiative you'll want to show," Kiki said before disappearing.

"Some initiative," Callie grumbled. "I mean, I *made* my entire outfit, and nobody seems to notice."

"Really?" Nadine asked. "That *ultra*-feminine fashion editor, Jorge, totally complimented me when I walked in. It seems nobody can resist me."

"You both look hot," Ava interrupted, "but these magazines aren't going to mail themselves."

They spent the next hour in focused silence, as they

wrote out address labels to luminaries like Demarchelier, Karan, Armani, Gisele. It was definitely grunt work, but somehow, *Couture* trusting them with the personal details of all of these fashion giants made Ava feel inexplicably as if she'd arrived—somewhere. Though she wasn't exactly sure where that might be.

Kiki returned an hour later, a mailroom attendant trailing behind, who grabbed the stack of envelopes and disappeared. Kiki eyed the remaining boxes. "Nadine, you finish the rest of these and then report to the photo department—you can help them with research for the Botox feature. Callie, you be a dear and go fetch some coffees. We have an ideas meeting after lunch, so everyone's a little stressed. Go around taking orders. You might need to make a few trips. And, Ava, I need you to help me with an article. We're doing a piece on the hottest new lingerie lines. We want something raunchy, like Agent Provocateur, paired with something sweet: think Sophie Simmons. And a rundown of the hottest shops for custom-made bras, panties, et cetera in New York, Miami, Los Angeles, and Chicago. Places the world doesn't know about. Insider secrets, you know, where Cameron, Scarlett, and Halle get their pretties. The equivalent of Sabia Rosa in the States. And be sure to check thefashionistablog.com, that blog everyone is buzzing about, too—if there's any gossipy insider dish to be had about lingerie, the Fashionista will have it."

Ava was furiously scribbling, trying to take down everything Kiki was saying, embarrassed that half of it sounded like Greek. When Kiki left, Ava groaned. And Nadine laughed.

"I'm sorry. I'm not trying to be a smartass," Nadine apologized. "But, Ava, you're not exactly up on the sexy."

"Tell me something I don't know," Ava said, feeling like a total failure. "I had no idea what she was talking about. *Saba Rose?*"

"Sabia Rosa," Callie said gently, placing a hand on Ava's shoulder. "It's this really ritzy lingerie place in Paris. Think of it as a fancy, frilly Frederick's of Hollywood."

"How do you know that?"

Callie shrugged. "I read a lot."

"I'll bet Aynsley's got some of that Parisian shit," Nadine interjected. "I'm telling you, that girl's walk-in closet is like a fashion museum."

"Yeah, well, plenty of girls at Bexley Prep shop at Sabia Rosa. It's overrated, if you ask me," Callie retorted. "We'd better get going, Ava." Callie flounced out of the office, and Ava turned, giving Nadine a close-range wave before following Callie's lead. In the hall, Callie confided in Ava. "Don't worry," she said. "I know of some really great places. One in Chicago, where I think Oprah gets her pajamas made, and they do these handmade bras and bustiers. Crazy expensive. There's also this place in Malibu I read about. I think Kate Hudson shops there like twice a week. And I can show you where to find out more."

"Really, you'll help me?" Ava asked in disbelief.

"Totally," Callie promised her. "But first, let's get the divas their skinny lattes before they carve our eyes out with their Jimmy Choos."

Three hours, four Starbucks runs, and two dozen phone calls and Google searches later, Ava felt like a minor expert on the world of high-end undergarments. With Callie's help, she'd drafted a memo to Kiki, outlining six of the hottest lingerie lines in the United States, London, Paris, and Japan, as well as six on-the-cusp-of-being-discovered boutiques. She'd cross-referenced which celeb was partial to which line and which store. Her head swimming with visions of Chantilly lace camisoles, satin champagne tap pants, lace demi-cup bras, and black leather garter belts, she handed over the dossier to Kiki, who arched an exquisitely plucked eyebrow as she perused the file. She read for a full five minutes. Ava felt her heart pound in anticipation, surprised by how much she cared what Kiki thought. And when Kiki declared the research "outstanding," Ava felt a blush of pride creep up her neck. She turned to Callie, who was sitting there poker-faced, obviously not about to take any of the credit that was rightfully hers.

"Thanks, Kiki. But honestly, I couldn't have done it without Callie," Ava admitted. "The girl has an ency-clopedic knowledge of fashion and celebrity trends."

Kiki trained her penetrating glance on Callie, as if seeing her for the first time. "Well, *brava* to both of you, then. You show this kind of initiative and you'll go far here. Much farther than fetching coffee. You girls should grab lunch," she added. "I'll see you at the meet-ing."

After Kiki had flounced off, Callie turned to Ava, a look of confusion and affection on her face. "You didn't have to do that, you know? I just gave you some names. You did all the legwork."

"But you *did* help me. It was only fair she should know how great you are," Ava said, smiling broadly.

Callie grinned back at her. "You're way too nice to make it in this industry," she said softly. "But don't change. Everyone else around here seems like such a shark—but I feel really safe around you. Like I can just be myself."

Ava felt a pang of something small and unpleasant, but it was quickly overshadowed by the warmth of her new friendship with Callie. "You can trust me," Ava said. And she wanted more than anything for it to be true.

5

Yves Saint Laurent: The Ultimate Power Suit

AYNSLEY MADE IT to the staff meeting with five minutes to spare, holding Polaroids of next season's Coach bags and Prada loafers high in her hand like some sort of fashion trophy. Marceline, *Couture*'s accessories editor, eagerly snatched the photos from her and patted for Aynsley to sit by her side.

Couture's senior staff was seated around the polished steel-and-glass kidney-shaped table. Aynsley was a little pleased to see that Ava and Callie were a row behind her, looking like scared schoolgirls sitting in folding chairs pushed up against the wall. Nadine, looking glamorous in Aynsley's Missoni, had nestled herself in next to the associate art director. When she saw Aynsley, her eyes widened in admiration and surprise. What had she expected? That Aynsley would crawl in wearing sweats, looking like yesterday's *foie gras*? Just the opposite. *Look good, feel good*, that was her motto. Which was why she'd specifically chosen to wear Yves Saint Laurent today. This hungover morning called for the ultimate power suit. The low-slung white trousers made Aynsley appear even lankier than she was, the creamy white fitted jacket dipped suggestively into her barely-there cleavage, and the suit's color perfectly off-set her raven hair. It also crossed her mind that sooth-ing white was the perfect antidote for the color explosion that was Nadine's outfit.

"You look hot!" Nadine mouthed.

"Thanks," Aynsley mouthed in return, regretting her cattiness. Nadine might be a tad *outré*, but the girl did play head games, a rare and welcome quality in Aynsley's world.

Kiki tottered in, collapsing into her seat dramati-cally. She was seated one chair over from the head of the table, where a glass of Chardonnay, glistening seductively, announced Isabel's pending arrival. Kiki appraised Aynsley and looked down at her own all-black ensemble. "Look at us. Ebony and ivory," she said. "Thanks for hitting all the showrooms for us. We've been trying to get into Coach for days, but Marceline hasn't had much luck, has she?" Kiki said, as if the accessories editor weren't sitting right there. Kiki eyed the rest of the room. "Nelson," she hissed at the copy chief. "Get rid of that can. Isabel hates Red Bull." Nelson quickly set the can on the floor beside his chair like a good little boy.

Dieter Glück arrived next, resplendent in a peg-legged pinstriped suit. Then, with a flourish, Isabel herself strolled in, taking the conference room's temperature up a notch. Isabel, a vision of chic in her pencil-slim gray Bottega Veneta suit, trilled, "September, September, September," as she slid into her chair. "August they forget, but September they remember." The staff giggled nervously, unsure what to make of Isabel's rhyming, but Aynsley guessed it meant she'd already had a bottle of wine with lunch. At Rothwell family dinner parties, Isabel's sense of humor always increased tenfold with every bottle of prosecco she downed.

"What do you have for me, *mes amis*? It must all be *parfait*!" There was a moment of uncomfortable silence before Isabel laughed, the staff following suit. "We shot two covers this month. Kate Moss looks radiant, and I love her Topshop line, but I am hesitant to have her with all her inevitable troubles," Isabel continued, touching her right nostril and snorting loudly. "We also had a shoot with Nanette Lise, who is suddenly this huge star in France, and oh so beautiful. The film of her is gorgeous, but no one here knows much of her yet."

"Isn't she starring in Spielberg's new movie?" Kiki interjected. "The film's already getting Oscar buzz. And it hits theaters in September, so the timing would be perfect."

"So, she is beautiful and in a movie. But is she interesting? Is she *Couture*? I'm afraid, even though she's my countrywoman, that I don't know enough of her."

"She's funny, smart, and totally wild," Aynsley piped up. "But, if that girl is twenty-one, like they said in *Variety*, then I'm a farm girl from Ohio."

Twenty-seven pairs of eyes suddenly trained on Aynsley, and Isabel cocked her head to the side, wanting more. Aynsley elaborated. "My brother dated Nanette. He met her in Saint-Tropez a few years back, and even *then* she was *at least* twenty-two."

The entire staff stared at Aynsley expectantly—especially Callie, who looked like she was about to fall out of her chair. Aynsley had them on the hook. "Jules likes to kiss and tell," she said with a mischievous wink.

"Anyway, at the time, Nanette had just graduated from the Sorbonne, your alma mater, Isabel," Aynsley continued. "She was bored, so she talked Julian into 'borrowing' Stavros Gianopoulos's yacht. They just marched on board, right past the crew, and she motored the thing around the harbor before the Coast Guard even noticed her. Of course, Stavros thought it was hilarious. Not long after, Nanette was dating *him*." Aynsley paused to laugh. "Jules had moved on to the next heiress by then."

Isabel clapped her hands in delight. "*Brava!* Can we go on record with that drama?"

"You didn't hear it from me," Aynsley said. "But I'm fairly sure there was an item about it in *Paris-Match*. And the Coast Guard probably filed an incident report, if you want to do some digging."

"Deanna's writing this, yes?" Isabel asked no one in particular. "Let's introduce her to Aynsley after the meeting. *Merci, ma chère*. How grateful we are for the Rothwell children. Now, onward. We have to discuss the Botox feature, and hair straighteners, and our wonderful Prague shoot, as well as finalize the Cutting Edge Designers Showcase. So much to do. And I need more wine."

• • • • • • • • • • • •

An hour later, Isabel declared the meeting over, naming Nanette Lise *Couture*'s September cover girl before rushing off to a standing appointment at the Red Door Spa. A group of staffers gathered around Aynsley, complimenting her YSL suit. "You'll have to give Julian a framed copy of our September cover," one of them said as Aynsley walked out of the conference room.

Elizabeth, the diminutive, perfectly coiffed beauty editor, followed Aynsley into the hall and pulled her aside. "Speaking of the September issue," she said, "I have an assignment for you. LuxeLife cosmetics is launching a new hair-straightening product. Their PR rep claims it's revolutionary—the at-home-equivalent of Japanese thermal reconditioning—but I have my doubts. Isabel wants to do an investigative thing, a kind of *Allure*-type beauty piece. I'd love for you to help with the research. I mean, obviously not on your own hair. It's perfect as is," Elizabeth said, gesturing to Aynsley's locks. "But have some of your friends try it out, and do some asking around to see if your set would even be willing to use an at-home treatment. It costs $200 a box, so it's not for Clairol users, if you get what I mean."

"I understand. Absolutely. Happy to help out." Aynsley smirked at Elizabeth.

"Fab," Elizabeth trilled. "Here are a few samples,

and the press materials. The shape of the article will depend on the results we get from your digging, so I need you to make it a top priority."

"No problem," Aynsley promised. "My day is wide open, now that I've done my showroom survey."

"Excellent."

Aynsley took the boxes and the sheaf of paper and dropped it on top of her iMac's keyboard. She kicked off her black Jimmy Choo slingbacks.

"Nice job, Sly," Nadine complimented her. "Clearly you do your best work hung over."

"Van Buren, you overestimate that hangover's power over me."

"Where'd you guys go last night?" Ava asked.

"Where *didn't* we go?" Aynsley replied.

"I dunno, but whatever we missed, let's hit those places tonight," Nadine said.

"I think it's all lame," Callie harrumphed.

Aynsley cocked her head to the side, her eyes glistening with faux sympathy. "What's the matter, Callie? Upset because you missed a good time, because you missed out on a plum assignment, or because Jules is out of your league?"

Callie shot a lethal look at Aynsley. "Well, if your brother *does* date me," she practically growled, "at least

I'll know it's because he likes *me*, and not who I *happen to know*."

"He'll appreciate who you are," Aynsley said dryly. "How sweet. And who exactly are you today?"

"Oh, you know *me*, Aynsley," Callie said with a self-satisfied grin. "I'm someone with *talent*. Someone who creates fashion, instead of just charging it on a credit card. And I have more to offer than my family's connections."

"Something tells me you think my brother's connections are worth quite a bit," Aynsley said, sounding perfectly casual. But she was simultaneously annoyed and unnerved. There was something off about Callie—her hunger, her eagerness, and her private school pedigree didn't mesh with her ra-ra-ra naïveté. Then again, the way she'd gone all vixen with Julian, maybe she wasn't so naïve after all. Aynsley suddenly felt tired from the day's exertions, not to mention her hangover which, in spite of what she'd told Nadine, had been hounding her all day. If she was expected to keep up with Nadine two nights in a row, she needed to rejuvenate.

"I'm out of here," she said.

"Where you going?" Nadine asked. "To test out hair straighteners?"

"Hardly. I'm hitting Balthazar for a latte, then Bliss

Soho for a pedicure. I'll meet you at Buddha Lounge at nine, Van Buren."

"Sure you can handle two nights in a row?" Nadine asked with a swagger in her voice.

"Oh, you've got no idea what I can handle," Aynsley said, before grabbing her brand-new Coach tote and heading out the door.

If you've got it, flaunt it.

Filed under: Fashionista > Style

For the price of a boob job? Buy a lifetime supply of <u>La Perla</u> push-up bras. *For the price of a nose job?* Look down your current nose through a pair of diamond-encrusted <u>Chanel</u> sunglasses. *And for the price of getting your thighs sucked?* Why not join an exclusive gym and work your booty out next to a hottie on a StairMaster? The truth is, my fellow fashionistas, learning to look fabulous the way you are is the best fashion investment.

Now, before you go thinking that the Fashionista has gone all earthy and soft, think again. I am not here to advocate for hairy legs (shudder the thought), or ugly clunky shoes. *Au contraire*, I'm all for looking gorgeous at all times. I believe you should never leave home *sans* <u>bronzer</u> and lip gloss. And only wear <u>sweatpants</u> if you're » planning to sweat. And, while yours truly has never let a plastic surgeon anywhere near her, I certainly can't fault <u>Ashlee Simpson</u> for her alleged little nose improvement. Notice I said *little*. But the Fashionista recently saw two models and one very well-known <u>Hollywood starlet</u> go too far under the knife. And it's not just the people who are paid to be pretty going wild, either. A certain editor at one of the top fashion magazines in the country just got back from a two-week "spa holiday" and had enough work done to shock <u>Dr. 90210</u>. I hate to break it to you, darlings, but reconstructing your whole bod won't make you look like a <u>supermodel</u> or a <u>Hollywood actress</u>— so why not work what you've got?

Your faithful Fashionista

6

Five-foot Diva with a Mile-wide Afro

NADINE KNEW, without a doubt, that Aynsley Rothwell had all the style *and* money that a girl could ever want—but when it came to luck, Nadine couldn't help but suspect that her friend had a little curse going. Because not five minutes after Aynsley had swanned out of *Couture* for her date with Bliss, Elizabeth, the beauty editor, returned in search of Aynsley.

Elizabeth was holding a purple folder embossed with LuxeLife in swooping cursive. She looked in the intern office and then toward the elevator, a frown creasing her well-preserved face. "Is that Aynsley I just saw heading for the elevators?" she asked.

The other interns' silence answered her question.

"Where'd she go?" Elizabeth asked. "Is she coming back?"

Callie smirked, her bee-stung lips twitching, but she somehow managed to keep quiet. The girl was so transparent; she couldn't even hide her schadenfreude. Nadine cleared her throat. "I think she, um, had to step out early, for an appointment."

Elizabeth rolled her eyes. "At four o'clock. How terribly professional. Who does she think she is? *Isabel?*" She turned to Nadine. "Here, you—what's your name again?"

"Nadine."

"Nadine. You do it. Read through this folder, then come to my office. I'll explain the assignment to you. And tell your little friend that she just made a wonderful first impression."

As Elizabeth flounced off, Nadine felt her own lips twitching into a smile. She bit them to keep the grin from showing itself. It wasn't cool to benefit from her friend's misfortune, but it was a little cool to score this plum assignment. Then Nadine looked at Callie, who was positively beaming. Nadine scowled. It was one thing for *her* to be happy. She'd scored the assignment and Aynsley was her friend—somehow that made it okay. But Callie's delight was bad form.

"Could you be a bigger bitch?" Nadine asked her.

Callie's smile turned to ice. "Whatever. At least I'm not backstabbing a friend."

It wasn't backstabbing. It was business. That's what Nadine told herself all the way downtown. To make herself feel better—and to look a bit hotter—she'd stopped at her dorm room for a costume change. When going out, *especially* out with a fashion plate like Aynsley, one had to look dazzling. Tonight she was wearing what Nadine liked to call a car-crash outfit—the kind of ensemble that guys got whiplash turning to look at: in this case, an orange-print Michael Kors halter bikini top and wrap skirt. It would have been perfect for a night of partying on the French Riviera. (At least that's what Nadine thought. Her European travels hadn't taken her any farther than Paris, and that was with parental supervision.) On her feet she wore five-inch copper platforms. And on her head, a huge blond Afro wig. By the time she'd finished primping, it was eight forty-five. The dorm cafeteria closed at eight. Oh well, she'd grab some food later on.

She arrived at Buddha Lounge at nine fifteen—her version of fashionably late—and descended a steep staircase into a cavernous room full of exposed brick, low-hanging chandeliers, woven bamboo walls, and smiling Buddhas. It looked like an exotic Asian palace, and the clientele seemed handpicked to complement the interior: sleek, modern, and excruciatingly laid-back.

She walked through the dining area, her stomach rumbling at the sight and smell of tantalizing plates of dim sum and other fancy Chinese foods. Some of the patrons gaped at her, mostly in a good way, except for one tight-ass bitch, who was sneering. *What was her problem?* Nadine thought. *Hadn't she ever seen a five-foot diva with a mile-wide Afro before?* She put on her best *I-own-this-place* face and finished a lap around the dining room. No sign of Sly, so Nadine walked past a series of smiling Buddhas in an arched hallway to the bar. She pulled up a stool next to some skinny, black-haired guy in an Agnès B suit.

"What's the bartender's specialty?" Nadine asked her neighbor.

"This is called a Heat," he said, holding up his orange-tinted glass.

"Heat. Well that sounds like a good drink for someone like me, don't you think?" She grinned, and the guy actually blushed. *Shit*—she thought New York guys were supposed to be tough, but so far they seemed like whimpering puppies.

"Hey barkeep. I need a little heat," Nadine called. The bartender looked down her bare torso and gave her a wink. Now that was more like it. Two minutes later, he laid a frothy concoction in front of her. She took a sip and coughed. "What's in this?" she said, fanning the air in front of her mouth.

"Chilies, plus tequila and Cointreau. And some cucumber," he added, "to balance the spice. Buddha was all about balance, you know."

"Right, and fifteen-dollar cocktails," Nadine joked.

The bartender laughed. "Do you want me to start a tab?"

"Uh, sure," Nadine responded, suddenly aware that she had about eight bucks in her wallet. Where the hell was Sly? Never mind her anemic wallet, Nadine wanted to explain what had happened with the LuxeLife assignment before she got too drunk to think straight.

Twenty minutes later, Nadine was still solo, nursing the dregs of her drink, and flirting like mad with the bartender because a) he was hot, if you went for the tall blond Adonis type, and b) in the event that Aynsley failed to show and Nadine was left with the bill, she would have to convince him to look the other way while she made a run for it. It seemed to be working. Ash—that was the hottie's name—asked Nadine where she was from and what she did, and he perked up when she told him that she was a photo editor at *Couture*. (It was almost true. Plus if she said she was an intern, he'd know that she was underage.)

Turned out Ash was a model. Big surprise. And, he said, turning up his dazzling grin, that he'd love to be in a *Couture* spread. *Fat chance,* Nadine thought. Anyone who actually read *Couture* knew that on the rare occasion the magazine ran a men's fashion feature, the clothes were modeled by celebrities like Clive Owen or Denzel Washington. Not that Nadine was gonna burst Ash's bubble, especially considering her bar-tab issues. She smiled till her cheeks ached and thrust her chest forward, which seemed to work because the next thing she knew, Ash had placed a "Heat on me" in front of her. Then he asked for her number.

She was practically through her second drink—the fiery sweetness of which had grown on her—when Aynsley breezed in. She too had changed for the evening. She looked like she'd poured herself into a pair of super-skinny True Religion jeans. On top, she wore an expensively simple silk camisole that was so sheer, you could just make out the silhouette of her tiny boobs. Her newly pedicured toes glistened from a pair of lizard-skin strappy high-heel sandals, and her hair was piled into a messy bun atop her head—all the better to show off the chandelier earrings dangling to her shoulders.

As Aynsley made her way over to the bar, heads swiveled toward her, like sunflowers leaning toward the sun. Nadine realized that most girls would be too intimidated to hang out with a girl like Aynsley, afraid that she'd suck up all the attention wherever she went. But Nadine wasn't like most girls. She knew damn well that she could hold her own with Sly, and *against the two of them together*? No one—certainly not Ava or Callie—stood a snowball's chance in hell.

"Ready for a cocktail?" Nadine asked as Aynsley plunked herself down on the barstool next to Nadine, which the guy in the Agnès B suit had vacated on her behalf.

Aynsley eyed Nadine's almost-empty glass. "Looks like you've had a head start," she said with a smirk.

"Two of them, actually. And the bartender asked for my number," Nadine bragged.

"Oh, Ash? He's such a himbo," Aynsley confided. "Word about him is that once you sleep with him, the free drinks stop, and the, you know, itching starts."

"Sly, that's disgusting," Nadine said, cracking up.

"It's the truth. He's a total—oh, hey Ash," Aynsley said, her smirk on full tilt.

"Hello, gorgeous," Ash greeted her. "Martini tonight?"

"A glass of Sauvignon Blanc, please," Aynsley replied. "I'm doing a detox diet."

"Since when?" Nadine scoffed.

"Since today. I decided to get a massage at Bliss, and my therapist said she could feel some toxin buildup. So now I'm cleansing."

"Oh, you are, are you?" Nadine asked, pointing to the white wine.

"It's white. It's light. Now, shall we inspect the merchandise?" Aynsley scrutinized the room, her eyes focused like laser beams. "See over there in the white linen suit? That's Alistair Griswold, as in the Griswold wing at the Met, as in one of the hottest bachelors in the city. Except he's gay. No one is supposed to know, but of course everyone does. Over there, in the silver slip dress, Lola Vladovic. Next to her is Svetlana Lybosky. Lola's Czech. Svetlana's Russian. They're on the verge of becoming the latest It models. Lola's got a Calvin Klein campaign launching, and Svetlana is Ralph

Lauren's new girl. They've been best friends for ages—people in the business call them 'The Eastern Bloc.'"

Nadine listened as Aynsley filled her in on the whole room. She was like an *E! News* reporter on autopilot, and she kept up her narration even as friends and admirers dropped by to air kiss. Nadine was sure that plenty of people, especially her Philly friends, would be quick to write off Aynsley: *over-privileged rich bitch*. But Nadine knew better. And not just because the girl was so charitable with her dad's credit card and her wardrobe. The way Aynsley took in the entire place at once and analyzed every designer outfit with a viciously clear head—that was some kind of gift.

Aynsley called for the tab. "My massage really loosened me up. I'm in the mood to move. I told some people we'd meet them at Bacchus for a quick drink and then we're going dancing."

"Sounds great," Nadine said. "But what about dinner?"

"I had some vile vegan raw thing. Part of the detox plan," Aynsley explained. "Didn't you order anything here? The food's fantastic."

Nadine shook her head, not about to tell Aynsley her bar-tab concerns. "I haven't eaten anything but the sandwich I grabbed from Le Pain Quotidien this morning."

"Don't worry, we'll get you something," Aynsley promised her. "Now drink up."

Two hours later, Nadine was smooshed in the backseat of a Lincoln Town Car, sitting on the cozy but unfamiliar lap of a guy named Spencer, who sat next to another guy named Hayden. Or maybe she was sitting on Hayden's lap, next to a guy named Spencer. She was way too plowed to tell. They were both hot, though. Both had brown hair and blue eyes, and both looked like they'd just stepped out of an Abercrombie & Fitch catalog. Nadine would've had a tough time telling them apart even if she were sober. They'd met the Bobbsey twins—old pals of Sly's—at Bacchus. Now they were all on their way to some dance club on Bowery. Nadine still hadn't eaten. At this point, plugging food into her alcohol-saturated system would be like pouring a tiny bottle of Evian into the Sahara— pointless.

Hayden/Spencer pulled out a silver hip flask, took a pull, and handed it around. Aynsley begged off, claiming, as she had all night, that she was detoxing. Now she'd even switched from white wine to Pellegrino. Whatever. Nadine planned to keep up with the big boys. No sissy-assed detox diet for this girl. The only thing stronger than her insides was her will. She grabbed the flask, engraved with the initials H.T.—which meant it was Hayden next to her and Spencer underneath her—and gulped.

"Atta girl," Hayden said, patting her on the thigh. "Take your medicine."

"Oh, baby, I don't need medicine," Nadine corrected him. "I am fine as is."

"Hey, back off, man," Spencer said. "She's on my lap."

"Now boys, there's enough of me to go around," Nadine said before first planting a drunken kiss on Spencer, then turning around the other way to smooch Hayden. "See. I'm good and plenty."

"Van Buren, don't be so generous," Aynsley said, trying to sound scolding.

Nadine looked over at Aynsley. Her hair had come undone from her bun and was hanging down around her face, but there was no missing the look behind her smirk: grudging admiration.

"Don't mind Miss High and Mighty over there," Nadine said, motioning to Aynsley. "She pretends to be all shocked, but deep down she needs to be around me. You see, Sly's got a wild girl locked inside her—and yours truly is her key."

To that Aynsley's smile went from a smirk to an embarrassed grin. "You may actually be right, though according to Gregory and Cecilia, I'm sufficiently wild."

"Nah, that don't mean a thing," Nadine said. "They just think you party too much, but c'mon, next to me, you're a nun. And they're just ignorant. I can tell—you are a girl wanting to break out, to show the world that there are some serious smarts behind that painting of a face you've got."

"Aynsley Einstein," Spencer/Hayden joked.

"Come on, dude. Don't get in the way of their Lifetime moment," mocked Hayden/Spencer.

Nadine iced them with a look. She wasn't kidding. Maybe it was the booze turning her sentimental, but Nadine had a feeling that Aynsley was like a little girl who needed a hug to make her skinned knee all better. She was about to say something else, but the Lincoln lurched to a stop. Nadine was pulled onto the sidewalk, past another velvet rope, and into a swirling cavernous club, where the beats and lights were thrumming in time. Hayden/Spencer gave her the flask again, but this time Aynsley grabbed it. "I'll take that. Here, you should eat this," she said as she thrust a peanut butter Luna bar at Nadine.

Nadine grabbed the snack and thanked Aynsley. As the guys pulled her toward the dance floor, she wondered if maybe she should've mentioned something about the LuxeLife assignment.

The next morning Nadine barely made it to the *Couture* offices on time. Her hangover was so severe that it made the previous morning's headache feel like a back rub. It had taken every ounce of her willpower to drag herself out of bed, shove her face under the faucet, and drink. She dressed in the least constricting outfit she owned (an uncharacteristically loose DKNY linen dress) and staggered into *Couture* a few minutes past ten. Even Callie looked like she felt sorry for her.

Luckily, most of the staff was too caught up yammering about the latest Fashionista blog to notice. In her compromised state, Nadine could barely keep the story straight, but apparently there was a veiled reference in the blog to a *Couture* editor who'd had a bunch of cosmetic surgery done. Staffers were debating whether it was Dieter or a fashion editor named Chiara.

Nadine was massaging her temples, feigning interest in the hubbub when Aynsley waltzed in at ten thirty, looking fresh as a daisy. She wore a yellow-and-white

Gucci sundress, paired with little white sandals and a tiny white handbag, an ensemble that was so sweetly retro, she could've worn white gloves with it. At first Nadine was perplexed—the girl had been so hung over the day before, and they hadn't partied nearly as hard their first night out. Then again, Nadine seemed to recall that Aynsley hadn't really had that much alcohol last night. Which was weird because she definitely encouraged Nadine's cocktail consumption—at least until they got to the last club. At that point Aynsley suggested Nadine drink some water, to which Nadine recalled bellowing, "No turning back now." That was right before she downed a tequila shot. *Ugh.* That tequila shot. It hurt just thinking about it.

Aynsley turned the same scrutinizing look on Nadine that she'd used on the Buddha Lounge patrons the night before—only this time, her face was sympathetic.

"You okay? You look better than I feared," Aynsley whispered.

"That's good. I'm dying inside," Nadine replied.

"I thought you might be. My mother gets migraines. I brought you some of her painkillers. They work really well and they won't make you drowsy. Have you had any coffee yet?"

Nadine put a hand to her mouth and shook her head. "Can't keep a thing down," she said through her fingers.

"Try," Aynsley whispered, handing over her own Starbucks cup. "It's a double latte. The caffeine will help your headache and the milk will settle your stomach."

"Thanks, Sly," Nadine said, some of her resentment receding. "And there's something I forgot to tell you about yesterday—"

As if on cue, Callie barged up to them, a look of obvious delight on her face. "Did you hear you lost your 'plum assignment'?" she asked Aynsley, making quote marks in the air with her hands.

"What are you babbling about?" Aynsley asked her, looking irritated.

"Oh, didn't your little buddy tell you?" Callie faked a look of concern. "Elizabeth was totally pissed that you skipped out yesterday, so she gave it to Nadine. You're on Starbucks duty today!"

Nadine felt a sudden pang of guilt.

"Is that true, Van Buren?" Aynsley asked, a touch of color warming her pale cheeks.

Nadine grimaced. "Yeah. I meant to tell you last night, but in case you didn't notice, I was a little drunk."

Aynsley's face went hard and angry, but her ire wasn't for Nadine; it was focused directly on Callie. "Perhaps you should worry a little more about your own career, Callie. Maybe think about cultivating a skill—something other than ass-kissing. Because you can't possibly think that wearing your work to the office is going to get those home-ec projects you call designs into the pages of *Couture*, can you?" Aynsley laughed, as though the notion of seeing a Callie Ryan design in *Couture* was the most comical idea she'd ever heard. "If that's what you're hoping," she added, "then you're even more deluded than I thought."

Callie opened and closed her mouth like a fish, turned on her heel, and flounced off, muttering "bitch" under her breath as she went.

Aynsley sighed. "That girl is working my last nerve."

"I'm sorry, Sly," Nadine said.

"What are *you* sorry for? I messed up. As predicted."

"Don't say that," Nadine protested. "It was nothing."

"That's big of you—especially after I encouraged you to get completely wasted last night—but it's true"—Aynsley shrugged—"I totally screwed up."

Nadine allowed herself a smile. Even that was painful. "Maybe you screwed up a little bit," she admitted.

"You know, you were right about what you said last night—about me wanting to break out." Aynsley sighed, and for the briefest instant Nadine glimpsed the fragile little Rothwell princess she'd had a hunch about. "But don't worry about me, Van Buren. I just have to find something to break in to."

7

The Ultimate Fashion Faux Pas

AVA STARED AT the screen of her iMac, her eyes crossing from trying to distinguish one patent leather satchel from the next. After her success with the lingerie assignment, Kiki had asked her to research ballet flats. Then, after declaring herself delighted with the results, she'd moved Ava on to bags, instructing her to go through the fall photo archive and highlight new and unusual totes, hobos, and satchels to be featured as the fashion editor's must-have picks.

At least she was on solid ground with handbags. Ava knew and loved bags. She owned several. Her lingerie collection, on the other hand, basically consisted of cute-but-common Calvin Klein bras and panties. She hadn't had anyone to wear sexy stuff for, much less to buy her anything wild, see-through, and cleavage-inducing.

Guys. Ava wasn't quite sure what it was about them, or about *her*. She knew she was pretty enough, prettier than plenty of girls who seemed to attract guys like moths to light. But Ava? She had a history of attracting men with ulterior motives—the kind of guys who didn't want *her* so much as something from her—but nice guys seemed to fly right past her. It was like she was invisible. Come to think of it, women didn't even seem to find her very memorable.

Which was what made Kiki's sudden faith in her so amazing. Because now Kiki wasn't just asking Ava to do research; she wanted her opinion. For the handbag assignment, Kiki had instructed her not just to go through the collections, but to highlight her favorite pieces. But how was she supposed to know if her favorites were good enough? If they were *Couture* enough? After three straight hours in front of the computer, Ava was on the verge of a major confidence crisis.

"Kiki said, 'pick the bags that speak to you,' but how do I know what's speaking to me? I'm not Kiki. Or

Isabel. Or you," Ava lamented to Callie.

"She wouldn't have chosen you if she didn't think you were up to it," Callie said, looking genuinely happy for her. It amazed Ava how Callie could switch her ambition on and off like that. Had it been Nadine or Aynsley who'd scored the purse assignment, Ava was pretty sure that Callie would've gone all glinty-eyed and sharklike.

"Easy for you to say, Little Miss Chic," Ava said, admiring Callie, who was wearing yet another one of her outfits. Today's Callie Ryan original paired a sexy sleeveless mod dress with a wide-lapeled jacket that had big cuffs and vintage crystal buttons.

"Do you like it?" Callie asked eagerly. "I think my look is evolving."

"It is," Ava confirmed. "You look great."

"*Thanks!* And *you* look hot in *that*," Callie said, pointing to Ava's BCBG sundress, splashed with a pretty tie-dye pattern. "You should show a little leg more often. You've got sexy stems."

"I'm glad you like them. No one else seems to notice," Ava mused. "Then again, I don't even know if any straight guys work at *Couture*."

"They do. Two of them, actually," Callie said with a devilish grin. "Owen in the mail room is definitely hetero, but he's got a girlfriend. And there's a total fox in the photo department—Sam, I think. I've been doing some homework on your behalf."

"What about on *your* behalf?" Ava asked, hoping to change the subject.

Callie flushed a little. "I've got my sights set elsewhere," she confided in a hushed voice.

Ava nodded knowingly. By the way Callie crossed swords with Aynsley over Julian, she could tell that Callie liked Julian for *real*—not just because she wanted to piss Aynsley off (although, that was a nice bonus). And from the way she'd seen Aynsley challenge Callie about her big brother, she had a feeling that Julian probably liked Callie, too. She wanted to tell Callie that, but her, *um*, limited guy experience didn't exactly qualify her to be a sage on relationship matters. "Back to purses," she said.

"Right. Purses. What kind do you like?"

Ava shrugged.

"Okay, well, what kind of bag are you carrying now?" Callie asked her.

Ava pointed to her tan canvas tote. "Not breathtakingly exciting, but dependable," she said, thinking that was how a lot of people would describe her *and* her bag. "I wanted to get one of those super-cute tropical-color hobos that are everywhere this summer, but—"

"You mean like this one?" Callie asked, pulling out a turquoise-and-apricot-striped hobo. She was grinning maniacally.

"Exactly like that one," Ava said with delight.

"I made this last summer. I was so ahead of the whole tropical trend," Callie bragged. She was staring at Ava's dress. "You know, this would go perfectly with your outfit. Look, the colors are almost an exact match."

"But isn't that a complete fashion faux pas—mixing stripes and tie-dye?" Ava asked, pointing to the swirls on her dress.

Callie smiled conspiratorially. "Let me tell you a secret about fashion. You can walk around in a skirt made of grass and a jacket made of burlap, and if you act like you're the hottest girl in the room, everyone will fawn all over you. It's all about the attitude."

Ava immediately thought of Aynsley, who looked amazing in whatever she wore. Granted, she had the perfect wardrobe, but Ava recalled the Eamon Sinds bag she'd carried to orientation: dark metal mesh, when everyone else was going for floral, and yet Aynsley wore it like it was the hottest accessory out there. Which it would soon be, Ava had no doubt. "You're right, as always," she told Callie.

"So here, the purse is yours," Callie offered.

Ava flushed with pleasure. "Seriously? I'll give it back at the end of the day."

Callie lovingly slapped her on the wrist. "Don't be silly. I'm giving it to you. I'll just borrow your bag for today and you take mine. Yours actually goes better with my outfit," she insisted. "But when you dazzle Kiki with *mine* at the staff meeting," Callie added, as she led Ava toward the conference room, "just don't forget to tell her it's a Callie Ryan original."

Ava sat through the staff meeting with excitement fluttering around in her stomach. It was the same feeling she'd had when she was addressing envelopes earlier in the week, like she was getting somewhere. And it would've been something delicious, something to savor, were it not competing with a small-but-growing knot of anxiety that seemed to dog her more with each passing day. The meeting itself was pretty mellow—at least by *Couture* standards. Just the daily check-in attended by section editors and Kiki. Isabel and the other heavy hitters didn't come, so Nelson was even drinking the verboten Red Bull. Unlike the last meeting, Ava and Callie were able to sit around the table this time. They sat with Nadine, who'd been looking a little off her game since yesterday, and Aynsley, who never appeared off her game—although she was definitely not the *bon vivant* she'd been at the last meeting. Aynsley ignored Callie but gave Ava a small smile, which made Ava feel, if not happy, relieved at the very least. She had enough going on without getting pulled into whatever drama was brewing between Aynsley and Callie.

After Kiki called the meeting to a close, as everyone else filed out, she ordered the interns to stay behind. "Some of you have proven quite able this week," she said, offering a simpering smile in Ava's vague direction. "Others, well, let's just say you'll want to raise the bar," she said, conspicuously *not* looking at Aynsley. "Summer Fridays in publishing are notoriously slow, so three of you may leave at four, while one stays until seven to put out any unexpected fires and answer Isabel's calls. She's already in the Hamptons and unlikely to need you, but that's beside the point."

Kiki had left it up to them to decide who would stay behind to cover the phones, and Nadine immediately looked at Ava, as if expecting her to volunteer her services. Normally, she would have. But today, Ava had counted on a short day—she had to leave by four. She was preparing to stammer out her excuse when Aynsley stepped forward. "I'll stay," she said, the curt tone of her voice preempting any objections or explanations.

So Ava left Nadine and Aynsley conferring in the hallway, probably about this weekend's wild plans, and hurried back to her desk. Callie caught up with her. "What do you want to do when we knock off work?" she asked breathlessly. "I thought we could cruise around Soho, or maybe even go to the poolside rooftop bar at the Gentry. See what all the fuss is about."

"Oh, sorry, Callie. I can't. I've got a doctor's appointment at four thirty," Ava explained.

"Why don't we meet at six, then?" Callie offered. "We can eat at the dorm and then hit some clubs."

"I'm going home to see my parents after that," Ava confessed. "I'll be on the seven o'clock train to Port Jefferson."

"When are you coming back?" Ava could hear the disappointment in Callie's voice. It made her feel totally guilty.

"Monday morning. I'll come straight to *Couture* from Long Island," Ava said, wincing to soften the blow.

"Oh," Callie replied, busying herself with an invisible piece of lint on her jacket. "I guess I'll fend for myself, then."

Ava felt bad about Callie, but she also felt the pressure of her four thirty appointment. She smiled, shrugged, and headed back to her desk. Callie sat down next to her. A minute later, the lanky receptionist came in. "You're Kelly, right?" she asked.

"Callie," Callie corrected her.

"Whatever. I've got a message for you. And would you please get your voice mail set up or ask your friends to call you on your cell," she said, clearly annoyed to be delivering phone messages to a lowly intern.

"It's probably my mom," she said, grabbing the pink slip. She looked at it, her eyebrows furrowing in confusion, then unfurrowing as a slow smile spread across her face. "It's Julian," she said in a dramatic whisper.

Ava could hear the echo of Nadine's booming voice coming from down the hall, followed by the quieter tones of Aynsley's breathy drawl. She gestured toward the hallway to warn Callie, who nodded in recognition and then disappeared into a nearby office.

"I'll be in the photo department," Nadine was saying as they approached the intern office. "Get me a mocha frappuccino please."

"Fine," Aynsley answered, turning to Ava. "I'm on coffee patrol for Kiki. Want anything?"

Ava was flattered by the offer, but she was nervous

enough without a caffeine infusion. "No thanks," she said. "I'm leaving once I finish my research."

"Bags, right? You should check out Dries Van Noten's collection. He's got some fantastic suede messenger bags for fall. Everyone I know is getting one. It's hilarious seeing all those Upper East Side matrons with messenger gear."

"Thanks," Ava said, grateful for the tip.

Aynsley disappeared into the lobby, and Nadine sauntered off toward the photo department. When the coast was clear, Callie poked her head out. She was pink, her face all aglow like she'd just run a race. "Are they gone?" she whispered.

Ava nodded, and Callie dropped herself into the chair next to her friend, and let out a long, happy sigh. "Guess who I'm going out with tomorrow?" she asked.

Ava put her finger to her cheek and tilted her head coyly. "Jake Gyllenhaal?" she asked.

"No."

"Tobey Maguire?"

"No!"

"Hmm. Could it be Julian Rothwell?"

"Yes!" Callie clapped her hands together like a little girl.

"That's so fantastic," Ava said, matching Callie's

enthusiasm. "Where's he taking you? And more importantly, *what* will you wear?"

"I don't know. But I have twenty-four hours to make sure I'm a knockout. He said we'd cruise around, maybe grab a bite. That means dinner, right? Who knows? Maybe we'll go to Per Se, or Nobu, or Masa. I've read about all these fabulous places, and now I'm going to get to eat in one! With Julian. God, Aynsley's gonna have a total shitfit when she hears this," Callie said, looking equal parts thrilled and scared by the prospect.

"I'm sure he'll take you somewhere fabulous."

Callie hugged herself with glee. "I'm going out with Julian Rothwell! Can you believe it?"

"Of course I can. Who wouldn't want to go out with you?" Ava asked. Callie was pretty, sweet, and sexy all at the same time. And she had huge talent. Once again, Ava felt the full force of her inadequacy.

Callie must have read Ava's thoughts somehow, because her look went from euphoric to sympathetic. "I am going to make you a promise, Ava Barton."

"Oh, really?"

"I am. By the time this summer is over, I'm going to find you a boyfriend."

Ava looked at her shoes. "That's a tall order," she murmured.

"No it's not," Callie retorted. "It's just a matter of making you realize how fab you are. And then we just pick a boy you think is hot, and *voilà*! Boyfriend."

"You make it sound so easy."

"It is. And trust me, once I've put my mind to it, I get what I want," Callie said, the metallic gleam of ambition back in her eyes. "Look, I landed this internship. I have a date with Julian. I'm going to get one of my designs into *Couture*. And I'm gonna find *you* a man."

8

Lipstick Stains—The Mother of Fashion Innovation

CALLIE DECIDED TO walk from *Couture* back downtown to the dorm. Her feet had mostly healed from the Sigerson Morrison disaster, and she'd quickly learned the New York working girl's best kept secret: Keep a pair of comfy-but-cute flip-flops with you at all times. Callie now never left home without her Ipanema Gisele Bündchen flops.

Besides, it was a beautiful afternoon, the air warm but not humid, and surprisingly fresh for the city. Callie planned to browse the shops on Broadway. She wanted to check out H&M's Roberto Cavalli collection. And Ava had mentioned a store called Daffy's that sold designer clothes at huge discounts. She also *had* to check out the windows at Macy's and some of the cute boutiques in the Flatiron district—solely for inspiration, of course.

Callie did a quick mental calculation of the funds in her savings account. Her parents had been supportive of her internship, had sprung for the dorm, airfare, and a small allowance, but Manhattan was not Columbus. They didn't have a clue how pricey things were. And besides, Callie was trying to cultivate a new image for herself, and that was expensive. Luckily, she had a secret weapon tucked away in her wallet: a Visa card. It was for emergencies only. But fashion emergencies counted, didn't they?

As she walked down Broadway, carried along in the bustle, Callie felt exhilarated. She was here. In New York. Working at the top fashion magazine in the country. Dating a hot guy, who just happened to be a socialite, or whatever the guy version of a Hilton sister was. She had this bubbling sensation that she really was going to make her mark. Callie Ryan wasn't going to be cowed by New York City. She was going to conquer it!

On 34th Street, she ogled Macy's windows, and then fought with the crowds to take the elevator up to Daffy's. It *did* look amazing, but she didn't feel up to weeding through the racks today. At H&M she picked up a pair of black satin tuxedo capri pants that emphasized her willowy figure and her tawny, toned calves. The pants would go perfectly with the white chiffon backless halter she was working on. Sexy and sophisticated—and only $35. She whipped out her charge card.

On lower Broadway she found a salon advertising a $25 mani-pedi. She stopped in and enjoyed a good scrub, pumice, and massage. She chose Vixen Red for her toes, and Essie Pinkadelic for her fingers. By the time she got back to the dorm, she was relaxed from the pampering, blissed out from her H&M score, and tingling with excitement over tomorrow.

All of which deflated like a popped balloon the minute she stepped into her room. The entire floor and both of the beds were strewn with Nadine's crap. There were piles of wild-printed skirts, skimpy camisoles, push-up bras, lace thongs, scarves, fishnet stockings, platform sandals, plus about a half dozen wigs and hair falls (which creeped Callie out on a good day). Most annoyingly, Callie's desk, the one where she kept her portable Viking sewing machine, sketches, projects, and all her swatches of fabric, was covered in a glittering array of cosmetics and hair products.

Surveying the messy dorm room, Callie felt her

anger rise from her stomach to her chest to her throat, which was so constricted she could barely speak. So she went to her desk, and with one sweep of her hand, smacked all of the jars and tubes to the floor.

"What the hell did you do that for?" Nadine demanded. It looked like she'd been napping; she was stretching her limbs, wearing a turquoise tank and matching boy shorts.

"Because your stuff was all over my desk!" Callie roared.

"Well, I didn't have any room on *my* desk, did I?" Nadine asked, pointing to her workspace, atop which were a laptop computer, three camera cases, and about five hats. "No need to throw a hissy fit."

"Are you kidding me? Look at this place! It's a total pigsty. Your crap is everywhere. I can't even see the floor. And on my bed. Oww!" Callie yelled, feeling a sharp sting penetrate her foot. She lifted it up to see a diamond stud lodged into her big toe. She flung the earring at Nadine.

"*Anal much?*" Nadine replied, her droopy eyes and her snooty tone infuriatingly blasé.

Callie was too enraged for words. She went around the room, flinging all of Nadine's mess onto her roommate's bed. That's when she saw the white chiffon halter on her sewing table, a gash of red across it. "Look what you did!" she yelled. "Do you know how expensive that fabric was?"

"It's just lipstick," Nadine scoffed. "You can Shout it out."

Callie felt on the verge of tears. But no way was she going to let herself cry. "What am I going to wear tomorrow?" she lamented.

"Tomorrow's Saturday. You won't see anyone from *Couture*, so what do you care?"

"Clean your shit up. Or I swear I'll throw it out the window," Callie warned, her voice a menacing growl.

"Whatever." Nadine bustled around the small room, piling on armfuls of clothes and dumping them into the closet. Callie heard her murmuring into her cell phone and then Nadine returned wearing short, tight cutoffs, and carrying a black overnight bag. "I'm crashing at Sly's pad for the weekend. She's having some people over. And I bet that hottie brother of hers will be there," she said, arching her eyebrow at Callie.

Callie was dying to brag that *she* would in fact be seeing Julian, and not just because he might drop by one of Sly's parties. But for some reason, she thought better of it and held her breath until Nadine flounced out the door.

Callie calmed herself by straightening up her part of the room and organizing her sewing area. Then she set about removing the lipstick stain with diluted rubbing alcohol and dishwashing liquid, her mom's secret formula. It mostly worked, but there was still a small patch of pink. She'd need to dry-clean it, but she wouldn't have time to do that and still wear it for her date with Julian. Just as she was contemplating a different outfit, she had a flash of inspiration. She pulled her tool kit out of her closet and, using wire and beads, she crafted a white beaded flower. The stain was right beneath the strap on the left side, and she sewed the flower over it. Then she tried it on. It was amazing. The flower somehow transformed the top from pretty to playfully elegant. Lipstick stains—the mother of fashion innovation!

It was ten o'clock by the time she'd finished doctoring up her top, and Callie was feeling a familiar thrum of adrenaline and inspiration. She pulled out her pad and started sketching. As was often the case these days, she was drawn to purses, tote bags, and shoes. All of them fabric-made. Callie knew her designs were good, but to make them spectacular, she had to find the right material. She planned to hit Chinatown, where she'd heard you could find lots of unique textiles.

She was up until two a.m. working, and without Nadine tromping around the place, she was able to sleep until noon the next day. Julian called shortly after she woke up and told her that he was going to take her to Brooklyn for the afternoon and dinner after that. Callie tried to hide her disappointment. She wanted to see Manhattan—not visit the hinterlands.

She spent the next hour and a half showering, straightening her hair, and buffing her body with exfoliants, lotions, and oils until it gleamed. She put on her new outfit, and was debating between shoes (sexy strappy black Kenneth Coles *or* comfy-but-cute Laundry ballet flats?) when Julian buzzed from downstairs. She slipped on the flats and was immediately grateful. Julian, after kissing her continental style, took her by the elbow and began leading her north on Broadway. *Great. More walking.*

"I thought we were going to Brooklyn," Callie said.

"We are."

"On foot?"

Julian grinned. "We're taking the subway. Williamsburg is just three stops on the L."

"Really, the subway? I mean, don't people like you take limos or cars?"

Julian laughed. "Maybe that's how it works where

you live, but here everyone from billionaires to bums take the subway."

"Oh, I knew that," Callie lied. "I was just teasing." She smiled to mask her grumpiness as they descended into the subway tunnels, muggy with the day's accumulated heat. But when the air-conditioned train arrived, she stole a long look at Julian. He was hotter than ever. His hair flopped over his sleepy, bedroom eyes. His butter-soft Levi's snug as a glove, and his woven T-shirt hinting at the contours of his wiry muscular chest. His battered leather Prada flip-flops showed off his tan feet and toes. Seeing them, Callie remembered he was supposed to be in the Hamptons.

She wet her lips into a sexy pout and cocked her head to the side. "How come you're not in the Hamptons this weekend?" she asked. "Don't you *summer* out there?" She'd recently heard Aynsley use the word "summer" as a verb and was practically giddy about having just used it herself.

Julian laughed, showing off his perfectly white teeth. "I was out during the week. Which I prefer. On weekends, every wannabe and poseur shows up. It's insufferable. Thankfully, I'm off to Europe soon." He said it so casually, the way Callie's mom might announce she was off to the mall.

"So where is it we're going?" Callie asked. "Williamstown?"

Julian slung an arm around Callie's shoulder. "You really are straight off the bus," he said with a laugh.

Callie scowled, making Julian laugh even harder. "Come on, Callie," he consoled her. "Don't be offended. That's what I like about you. Among other things," he added lasciviously. "It's Williams*burg*."

"So, what's so special about Williamsburg? Isn't Manhattan where it's at?"

"Maybe if you're a stockbroker or some hedge-fund stooge like my father," Julian explained. "But let's just put it this way: Brooklyn is the new Manhattan."

"So what's Manhattan, then?"

"It's a mall in Jersey. You've seen Times Square, right?" Julian asked pointedly. "It's all Disney neon and tourists in fanny packs. Williamsburg is edgy. It's where all the galleries are moving to. It's full of energy. Trust me," he added, "you'll love it."

Callie was skeptical, right up until the moment they emerged from the train. She looked around: Everyone was under the age of thirty. They all looked like they'd stepped straight out of a Beck video. The guys with their skinny jeans and bold black tattoos, the girls with funky shagged eighties haircuts, Jackie O sunglasses, and original style that paired, say, a seventies vintage polyester dress with a $500 Alexander McQueen jacket. It was like someone had taken the most wildly stylish parts of Manhattan and transferred them here. Callie was so enthralled that a mouth-gaping grin momentarily cracked her blasé mask.

Julian watched her and smiled. "I told you," he said affectionately. "Shall we cruise around? There are a few galleries I'd like to hit, then we can have a cocktail and grab dinner."

Callie nodded, her grin threatening to split her face. Julian took her by the hand. It felt less romantic, more like they were partners in crime, but either way, it was delicious. Callie traipsed after him as they went from one industrial gallery to the next, until the blur of white-bricked walls, abstract oil paintings, and avant-garde sculptures threatened to bleed together. Julian, for his part, was clearly in his element, schmoozing with all the gallery owners or, in many cases, the artists themselves. He seemed to know everyone, and everyone fawned over him. Especially, Callie noticed, the women. It was the kind of thing that normally made her jealous, but she couldn't help feeling triumphant (*she* was his date!). He usually hooked up with heiresses and famous French starlets, but today he was out with

Callie Ryan, even if he *was* acting more like an excited tour guide than a potential boyfriend.

In between visiting the galleries, they walked up and down the streets, and Callie drooled over shops that were similar to the kind of boutique she hoped to own one day—before she went multinational, of course. When Julian recommended they step into the Sarah Bowen Gallery to look at a group sculpture exhibit, Callie suggested that they split up for a bit so she could check out some boutiques. "I'm a designer, so I should size up the competition," she explained.

"You want me to come with you?" Julian asked.

Callie couldn't imagine any of the guys she'd dated in Ohio offering to go shopping. But to be honest, Callie would be too distracted with Julian at her side. She grinned her sexiest grin. "How about we meet in half an hour and grab a drink. I'm dying for a cocktail."

Julian looked at his watch. "Where are my manners? Six o'clock and I haven't even offered the lady a drink. I'll meet you out front at six thirty."

Callie hustled downstairs, rushing to take in as many places as she could. She went from boutique to boutique, and then found the mother lode: a renovated factory full of small designer shops and gourmet food stalls. She nosed around, in total heaven, until it was time to meet Julian. Just as she was about to leave, she spotted a flash of color and what she thought was the face of Marilyn Monroe. She came closer. It was a four-by-four-foot square silk screen of Marilyn Monroe's face; the way the color bled out in all directions made it look like an Andy Warhol painting, funky and hip. As she was admiring it, a beanpole of a guy wearing hipster-nerd glasses approached.

"Ahh, the Marilyn," he said.

"Wow! This is incredible," Callie gushed. "Did you make it?"

"Yep. I do these for fun, though most of my market is hats," he said, pointing to the wildly colored Dr. Seuss-looking hats adorning the walls of his stall. "If you like them, I've got more." He reached down under the counter for a box. Inside were at least a dozen silk screens, each of a different famous (and dead) person: Elvis. Kurt Cobain. Che Guevara. Tupac.

"Tell you what," the guy said. "I'll sell you the whole lot for a hundred bucks."

"For real?" Callie asked, the excitement growing in her stomach. She knew exactly what she wanted to do with them.

"Why not?" The guy shrugged. "You seem like a nice girl, and no one else wants 'em."

Callie grinned. "I'll take them. Do you take credit?"

• • • • • • • • • • • •

After drinks at Darwin, a cool, cavernous space with a reflecting pool, Julian led Callie back outside for dinner. "You're not a vegetarian or a raw foodist, are you?" he asked.

"Are you kidding? I'm from Ohio."

"Oh, that's right. Buckley. You go to prep school. Sly said something about that."

"Bexley," Callie said, quickly changing the subject. "So where are we going?"

"A surprise. But it's one of the best restaurants in the city," Julian promised her.

Callie was as excited as she'd been the day before, when she'd hoped for Union Square Café. All afternoon, they'd passed one gleaming eatery after the other, and Callie felt sure she'd be eating in the latest hot spot, a place that most other girls would only read about in *Us* weekly. But as they walked, the boutiques and cafés gave way to ugly tenements and 99-cent stores, until they reached their destination: Peter Luger's Steakhouse. For the third time that day, Callie was disappointed. A steakhouse? They had a zillion of those in Ohio. And this one was filled with ugly, long wood tables and ancient waiters in tuxedo jackets.

Julian must have read the look on her face, because once again, he laughed. "I take it you've never heard of Peter Luger's?"

Callie shook her head. "I know it doesn't look like much, but it's a meat orgasm. The best steak in the city," he promised her.

Callie realized later that she was just going to have to learn to trust Julian, because not only was the aged T-bone he ordered for them to share the most incredible thing she'd ever tasted—before the night was over, she'd spotted five A-list celebrities dining in the dimly lit restaurant.

After dinner, her stomach full of steak and creamed spinach, her shoulder bag stuffed with silk screens, she and Julian rode back to her dorm (in a black Town Car this time). On the ride home, Callie wasn't thinking about Julian so much as what she was going to do with her new fabric. Which was why, when he left her with no more than a chaste peck on the lips, Callie wasn't disappointed. In fact, as far as she was concerned, it had been the best date ever.

Brown paper packages tied up with string. These are a few of my favorite things.

Filed under: Fashionista > Style

I suppose that, like Maria from _The Sound of Music_, I do enjoy brown paper packages—especially when emblazoned with the words Sigerson Morrison.

A little admission: The Fashionista has had a bad couple of days. And when that happens, there is only one certain fix: a little retail therapy. Lately the place that makes the Fashionista happiest is Manhattan's Nolita neighborhood (that's an acronym for North of Little Italy for all you non-Gothamites). It's chockablock full of the most darling boutiques—like Le Marais in Paris, only hipper. And, the Fashionista scored so big » in Nolita today that she's compelled to dish about her fashion finds.

My first stop was Calypso, where I picked up the yummiest little ethnic throw, and my mood picked up, too. Then I skittered on down to INA—yes, the Fashionista shops at consignment stores . . . not for budgetary reasons; because it's the best way to exchange tired old clothes for something one-of-a-kind. Today, for example, I purged a D&G jacket from my closet, swapping it for a fab vintage Pucci dress. Added bonus: a Parker Posey spotting (FYI: Parker's the coolest actress in the entire city). Next stop was Lyell on Elizabeth Street, where I found the most glorious gold 1930s bias-cut sundress (that did wonders for my mood!). At Tory Burch, the Fashionista shopped alongside the two most famous celebrity twins in the world and also scored herself a sexy bias-cut dress to boot. Then it was off to Blue Bag, where a tiny leather satchel practically induced euphoria. I hit Poppy, just to see what the hot new designers are up to (hint: lots of fabulous and fun color); followed by Eva, because one must keep an eye on European designers as well. My final stops were the aforementioned Sigerson Morrison for the cutest ballet flats ever—and a tête-à-tête with an up-and-coming socialite-cum-handbag » designer at her atelier. Between the daily scores and exceptional company, the Fashionista's day was made blissfully glam. Hope yours is too.

Your faithful Fashionista

9

Beyoncé Stole My Hair

AT FIRST AYNSLEY had thought maybe she was being paranoid, but now her worst fears had borne out: Isabel and Cecilia were definitely colluding to "Teach Aynsley Rothwell a Lesson." How else to explain the increasingly demeaning errands she'd been sent on? Since last week, after the Bliss debacle, she'd been the official *Couture* Starbucks slave, hauling so many trays of frappuccinos and iced skinny mochas that the baristas now knew her by name. But had she let loose an ounce of attitude when Kiki handed her—*yet another*—order list? No. She had taken it with a smile (okay, maybe it was more of a smirk). And she hadn't spilled so much as a drop, no easy feat dodging 42nd Street's crowds in four-inch Jimmy Choo metallic sandals while balancing two trays of icy beverages.

This week, however, the errands smacked of hazing. *Pick up a copy of the new Philip Roth novel at Borders,* even though there was a Barnes & Noble two blocks away. *Hand deliver an invitation to the Cutting Edge Designers' Gala,* even though *Couture* usually hired a messenger service to handle things like that. *Take the subway to Nolita to search for the satchel Isabel read about in thefashionistablog.com*, even though stores across the city had sold out of the bag an hour after the blog had named it. *And today?* Aynsley had been called on her cell at seven thirty a.m. and ordered to pick up Isabel's *dry cleaning* before work—even though the dry cleaner was miles downtown in Tribeca, and a block from Isabel's loft.

The latest indignity had put her in such a foul mood that not even her new Tricia Fix Indian-print empire-waist dress could cheer her. Aynsley gritted her teeth as she pulled on the new dress, tied the straps of her brown leather lace-up sandals around her calves, and braided her long black hair into two plaits—she was cultivating a new *haute* Pocahontas thing. But her *look good, feel good* strategy couldn't quell the burning shame in her stomach, and once in the cab, she seemed to grow pissier with every passing block.

It was just so absurd! Aynsley Rothwell knew more about fashion than the other interns combined. And yet Ava was being tossed one research task after the next. Nadine was moving ahead on the straightening assignment. And Callie? With all her sewing prowess, that girl still had a knack for ruining a perfectly cute piece by pairing it with some hideous ruffled miniskirt and espadrilles. As far as Aynsley was concerned, murdering a stylish piece of clothing was even more of a fashion sin than wearing some god-awful Casual Corner outfit. Callie had no taste, at least not *Couture* taste, and yet not only had she been on a date with Jules—her brother obviously had taste issues of his own—but she'd spent all week ensconced in the fashion department. Callie had been helping to organize and pack clothes for the upcoming Cutting Edge Designers shoot, while Aynsley Rothwell was nothing more than a glorified errand girl.

Aynsley dutifully picked up the dry cleaning and returned to *Couture* where, in spite of her best efforts to remain resentful, she immediately felt better. The hallways with their rolling racks full of yummy designer wear, the duffels and trunks being packed for shoots, and the mockup board of this month's issue were her fashion therapy. They calmed and invigorated her, much the same way that diving off the dock into the Caribbean at the Four Seasons Resort in Nevis always did.

"Hi Kiki. Dry cleaning is in Isa's office. Want me to hit Starbucks?" Aynsley asked with forced enthusiasm.

Kiki cocked her head to the side. "Love the dress. Is that a Stella?"

"Tricia Fix. From her new collection."

"It's fabulous. Hey, check out my new bag." Kiki held up a tan-and-white buckskin number, petting it as if it were a kitten.

"You scored yourself a new Sinds," Aynsley noted with a smirk.

"His people sent over four bags. A thank-you for anointing him the hottest handbag maker in our Cutting Edge Designers feature. Isabel kept three, naturally, but I think I got the best one, don't you?"

"Absolutely," Aynsley said, neglecting to mention that she'd passed on the very same buckskin when Eamon had showed it to her in his London workshop. He'd confided that he thought mesh was the next big thing, and Aynsley was betting on Eamon.

Kiki beamed. "Will you do me a favor? We've got

an advertiser meeting with LuxeLife this morning. They're very unhappy with our coverage, something about not feeling the love." She paused to roll her eyes. "Elizabeth's on a shoot, so I have to attend in her place with one of the assistants. Can you come along? They'll feel important, as if they warrant a crowd."

"I'd be happy to." At least she was off coffee duty.

"Great. It's in my office at eleven," Kiki added, "so go catch up with your work and come by later."

"Will do," Aynsley agreed.

Back in the intern office, Ava was doing a Nexis search for a feature on female army officers. Callie was checking *Couture*'s general email account. Nadine, however, was nowhere to be seen. Which was strange. Even when she was crippled by a hangover, the girl was still prompt, and last night had been the first time all week that Nadine and Aynsley *hadn't* partied. Aynsley's uncle Presley was in town, and that meant an insanely dull dinner for the Rothwell offspring at the Yale Club. Nadine had said she was going to take the opportunity to shoot some pictures, maybe do a little *Couture* research—and, annoyingly, make things right with Callie. The roommates hadn't really been speaking since their state-of-the-dorm tiff. Not that they'd seen much of each other. Nadine had been working all day in the photo department and spending every night at the Rothwells'.

"I think I've got to make things straight with her," Nadine had told Aynsley the day before while nibbling on salads on their lunch break at Bryant Park. "It's been buggin' me. I mean, I did get lipstick all over her pretty white top."

"Just give her dry-cleaning money, and be done with it," Aynsley had suggested, wrinkling her nose.

"You're so cold, Sly." Nadine had laughed. "I might be stubborn, and I might be a slob—I *know* I'm a diva—but I'm not above apologizing when I'm wrong."

Aynsley looked around for Nadine again, and then checked her BlackBerry. Nothing. "Anyone seen Van Buren?" she asked casually.

"She called. She's running late," Callie answered without looking up from her computer. "Some sort of minor emergency."

So they *had* made up. How sweet. Aynsley swallowed her annoyance and asked, "Did she go out with Hayden or Spencer last night?"

"Nope," Callie said, still staring at her computer. "We all had dinner at the dorm together and then hung out in Washington Square while she took pictures of all the freaks. We had fun, didn't we, Ava?"

"Yeah. We missed you, though," Ava said diplomatically.

"How nice. I take it you two and Nadine are simpatico," Aynsley asked, unable to control the sarcasm.

Callie beamed the world's fakest smile at Aynsley. "Like sistas," she said.

Aynsley cringed. *Sistas?* Did Callie actually think that Aynsley would be jealous because they'd all eaten turkey burgers and frozen yogurt sundaes in the cafeteria together? Because Callie had been Julian's flavor of the week? She glanced at her Dean leather bracelet watch and saw that it was almost eleven. Thank god.

"Time for Starbucks?" Callie gloated.

"Actually, I'm off to an advertiser's meeting with Kiki. *Ciao,*" she said, allowing herself a moment to savor the flash of envy in Callie's hazel eyes.

The fact that Callie was jealous was about the only thing the LuxeLife meeting had going for it. The proceedings were unbearably dull. The president of LuxeLife—not some foxy glam hipster but a balding middle-aged guy—and his birdlike PR rep spent the whole time simultaneously gushing to Kiki about

Couture's market dominance, and complaining that the magazine gave more play to cosmetics companies like Fresh and Clé de Peau. Kiki politely explained that *Couture* readers demanded to know about the latest high-end age-defying creams, which those companies made and LuxeLife did not. "But we certainly do cover your adorable lipsticks and nail polishes, and your hair tonics," Kiki said.

"Well, that's simply not enough to justify what we spend on ads," the PR woman said with a sniff.

Aynsley could tell Kiki was getting flustered, so she jumped in. "Aren't we considering a feature on Luxe-Life's new hair-straightening treatment, StraightEdge?" Aynsley asked.

Kiki shot her a look of pure gratitude and gave the beauty assistant a barely perceptible sneer: She *so* should've spoken up about that.

"StraightEdge, as its name implies, is the edge of the cutting edge in hair care," the bony PR woman droned as if reading from a script. "Women who are now paying upwards of a thousand dollars a treatment will be able to achieve the same effect at home for two hundred dollars."

What Aynsley *didn't* say was that *Couture* readers didn't want cheap alternatives. They wanted to be the first to know about the next *two-thousand-dollar* hair treatment so that they could get it before all their friends did and score bragging rights. What else did these people not understand?

Kiki would have agreed with Aynsley, but she was in full-on BS mode, yammering about how *of course* this treatment could be revolutionary, and that *Couture* was in the process of putting it through rigorous testing. All of which made Nadine's arrival on the scene a case of incredibly bad timing.

When Nadine burst into the room, her mocha face was flushed pink, her eyes were makeup-less and red-rimmed, and her chest was heaving with such force that her boobs were practically falling out of her pink-and-black netted Betsey Johnson dress. Her long, kinky reddish-brown hair was gone, replaced by a chic pixie cut that Aynsley thought flattered her friend's high cheekbones and almond-shaped eyes.

"Nadine, we're in a meeting," Kiki said sternly.

"Your meeting can wait. Look at my hair!" she wailed.

"It looks fantastic," Aynsley said, trying to talk Nadine down from whatever cliff she seemed about to jump off of.

"Are you kidding me? It's a scabby, nappy nightmare.

I look like Beyoncé stole my hair. And you wanna know why? Because I used that crappy straightener. Not only did it sting like a son of a bitch—I've got scabs on my scalp to prove it—but it singed my hair off in chunks. I had to chop the rest of it off this morning."

"Nadine," Kiki interrupted, in her iciest voice. "We'll discuss this *later*."

Nadine didn't seem to hear Kiki's words or the dangerous edge in her tone, because she barely took a breath before ranting some more. "I can't believe you guys gave me this product to try. I mean, this is *Couture*. I assumed it would be safe and it practically burned my head off. LuxeLife my ass. More like SucksLife."

"Nadine!" Aynsley raised her voice as loudly as she could without shouting. "Shut up."

"I won't shut up. My hair is part of my look, it's—"

"Nadine, this is Paul Mathiason, the head of LuxeLife cosmetics," Kiki said, looking as though she wanted to strangle Nadine.

For the first time in two weeks, Nadine Van Buren was speechless. Her jaw dropped. Her face paled two shades, and she looked at Kiki and Aynsley with equal parts fury and mortification. Then she backed out of the room without a word.

The LuxeLife team glared at Kiki, who was rubbing her forehead, looking suddenly exhausted. The beauty assistant scrutinized her shoes with great interest.

"Don't mind Nadine, Mr. Mathiason," Aynsley jumped in. She turned toward the portly cosmetics exec and his pinch-faced companion. "That girl's hair is so fried from all her treatments, I'm sure baby oil would've snapped it off. If ever there was someone who could benefit from LuxeLife RevitaLocks, it's Nadine. I think your straightener is fantastic, by the way. You can see that it transformed my wavy hair to stick straight without a hitch." She waved a braid at them.

"You used StraightEdge?" the PR woman asked.

"Of course. That's why I'm in the meeting, right, Kiki?"

Kiki nodded and swallowed, relief inching its way across her nervous face.

"Obviously, we can't really tell you about our testing process until it's complete," Aynsley continued. "But I wouldn't worry about Nadine. She's a tad dramatic." Aynsley laughed her most charming giggle. "And very green. She's an intern."

"An intern?" The PR woman asked. "Why would you let an intern test our products?"

Kiki looked alarmed again. Aynsley sighed and

stepped in. "We feel it's important to gauge a product's appeal in the youth market."

Mr. Mathiason clapped his hands together. "Excellent thinking. The kids are the future, that's what I always say. I think we're done here. We'll look forward to hearing more of what smart editors like this young lady have to say about StraightEdge, and we'll be doing another six-month ad buy."

"Excellent," Kiki said, smiling broadly. She quickly ushered the LuxeLife team through *Couture*'s hallways and toward reception before scurrying back to intercept Aynsley. "How amazing were you? They ate it up. Good girl. You probably saved the magazine from losing a couple hundred grand in ad revenue. I'm going to inform Isabel right now."

"Please don't," Aynsley said.

"Why ever not?"

Aynsley wasn't quite sure how to answer that. Maybe it was because she didn't want Isabel, and by extension, Cecelia, to hear that she'd succeeded by lying through her teeth. Or maybe it was something else. She wanted her success or failure at *Couture* to be hers, and not some parental report card. "Oh, I'm sure *you* can understand, Kiki."

Kiki looked mildly perplexed, and then immediately forgot about it. "Of course. But. I'll tell you one thing—you're off Starbucks duty. Permanently. And your buddy Nadine? She'll be lucky to have any hair left at all by the time I'm finished with her."

10

Ultra Limited Edition

BRRR-ING . . . BRRR-ING . . . *Brrr*-ing.

"Goddammit, someone answer the phone," Nadine screamed.

Callie, Ava, and Aynsley all stared at Nadine and simultaneously rolled their eyes.

Nadine raised her hands as if in surrender. "I'm sorry, but I swear if Kiki calls one more time I'm gonna lose it."

Couture was in chaos. It was Thursday afternoon and there were two separate last-minute location shoots happening in the city for the giant August Cutting Edge Designers Showcase—a forty-page *Couture* feature highlighting the twenty hottest new clothing, accessory, and jewelry designers. This would be enough to set Kiki off on a good day, but complicating matters was the heat wave that had descended upon New York City, driving the mercury to the high 90s. The models showing off the hottest—literally in this case—coats in Central Park were melting, and one of the girls on set at a shoot in Brooklyn's cobblestone-lined DUMBO district had been rushed to the hospital for heat stroke.

All of which was giving Kiki a stroke of her own. She'd ordered all the interns off their previous projects, commanding them to await her every call. And call she had. Every ten minutes for the last several hours, issuing increasingly panicked demands: run down to Click to get the latest portfolio of some Hungarian model who *might* sub for the sick model; go to DUMBO to deliver the chunky silver belt Dieter had forgotten; order blocks of ice to be delivered to Central Park; call her dog's day care center to make sure BoBo wasn't being walked in this heat.

The phone was still ringing. Ava shrugged helplessly and picked it up. She listened, murmuring okays before saying her good-byes.

"Kiki again," Ava said. "One of the models is a vegan and wants a portobello mushroom sandwich and sweet potato fries. Another is demanding a watermelon fruitsicle and they only have cherry. I'm supposed to get the stuff and cab it up to the park. Who does a good portobello burger?"

"Eatery on Ninth Avenue," Aynsley suggested.

"Unbelievable," Nadine said with the world's most dramatic sigh.

"I don't get what you're bitching about," Callie said. "After more than two weeks, we're finally seeing some action today." Callie, for her part, had just returned from running up to the Central Park shoot. She'd been amazed by all the people on set: stylists, hair and makeup people, the photographer, her assistants, the creative director, the photo director, and the fashion editors. And then there were the models. Callie never imagined she could feel sorry for the leggy beauties, but seeing them sweltering away in wool and leather— "Well, I was sure glad I wasn't one of them," Callie told Ava. "They were suffering. Even though they were wearing ice compresses under their coats, and they had these little tents set up with lamps that sprayed cool mist. I was grateful I was wearing this," she said, pointing to the cotton red-and-white-striped Paul & Joe spaghetti strap dress that she'd picked up for $54 at Century 21 (*the* most amazing discount department store she'd ever been to—although she was not about to admit to anyone but Ava that she shopped for discounts).

"Aren't we protected by any labor laws?" Nadine asked. "It's an inferno out there, and the editors are sitting in their air-conditioned offices while we hustle all over town doing *their* dirty work."

"Wrong, Van Buren," Aynsley corrected her. "They're making the three of us do *their* dirty work. They're making you do *our* dirty work."

Callie had noticed that ever since the hair incident, Nadine's chores had been so ridiculous they'd made Aynsley's earlier hazing look like a cakewalk. Today, for instance, Kiki had specifically ordered Nadine to get the blocks of ice delivered up to the park (much harder than you might think), call BoBo's doggie day care (twice), and after lunch, get Kiki a last-minute appointment for a Lifting Facial at Shizuka. While spa directors would open their doors in the middle of the night for Isabel, Kiki didn't have quite the same pull. Nadine had been forced to trudge through Midtown's boiling streets all the way to the Zen day spa to plead in person with the spa's snooty manager.

"Piss off, Sly," Nadine said grumpily.

"Now, now," Aynsley retorted, looking annoyingly cool in her lime green Vivienne Tam '60s-inspired sheath. "Your big mouth is part of what got you into this fix in the first place."

"Bullshit," Nadine protested. "It was LuxeLife's lame-ass product."

"I'll bet the product works fine if you take it off after twenty minutes," Callie said. "You left that weird shower cap thing it came with on for like an hour when you fell asleep." She tried not to laugh, even though it *was* pretty funny. She really did feel bad for Nadine, first for losing her hair and then for having shoved her foot in her mouth at the LuxeLife meeting.

Plus, Nadine had been a lot friendlier lately, and she'd been really supportive of the bags Callie was making out of the silk screens she'd bought in Williamsburg (a project that had been monopolizing most of Callie's attention). She'd worked the entire Sunday after her date with Julian, sketching out her designs, and had rushed home after work to get started sewing them on Monday. She'd even brought a few bags into the office to work on during down time.

"The LuxeLife people probably don't recommend naps." Aynsley laughed.

Callie hid her smile. Maybe it was the heat, but Aynsley had retracted her claws.

"God, I'm sweating even in the AC," Ava said, fanning her black sheer silk Calvin Klein top and twisting her hair into a bun. "I'm tempted to buzz my hair just like Nadine's. Give me the scissors." Ava reached for the shears.

"Don't you dare," Callie said. "Long hair is sexy. That's why guys love it."

"What are you saying?" Nadine demanded.

"Oh, chill out," Aynsley said. "They love boobs, too, and you've got those in spades."

"Damn straight," Nadine said, shoving out her chest so that it strained even further against the fabric of her orange Adam+Eve halter top.

"And you still have all your wigs, so you can have long hair whenever you want," Callie reminded her.

"It's too hot for a wig," Nadine whined.

"She's right," Ava replied. "Let's all do buzz cuts." She reached for the scissors again and pretended to go after Callie and Aynsley, who shooed her off. They all laughed until their eyes were tearing.

The ringing phone interrupted them. Nadine groaned and rolled her eyes. "Yeah, Kiki," she said as she answered the phone, not even bothering to mask her annoyance.

"Way to impress," Aynsley whispered, shaking her head.

"Oh, hello," Nadine said, clearing her throat, and sitting up straighter in her chair. "I just hung up with her and thought . . . no, she's here. Uh-huh. I'll send her over now." Nadine gently returned the phone to its cradle and turned to look at Callie.

"Great. What's my chore?" Callie asked.

"That wasn't Kiki," Nadine said, looking shell-shocked. "It was Isabel," she explained, uttering the editor's name in a reverent whisper.

"You mean her assistant," Aynsley corrected.

"No. I don't mean her assistant. I mean Isabel Dupre." Nadine turned back to Callie. "She wants to see you in her office *now*."

Callie felt a jolt of fear, like she'd just been summoned to the principal's office. Was she going to get fired? Had Isabel found out that she'd lied about Bexley Prep? That she'd been working on her bags in the office? That she owned a closet full of Marc Jacobs knockoffs? As she contemplated different scenarios, her hands grew moist with sweat.

She looked to Ava and Nadine for reassurance, but they seemed as freaked out as she felt. Aynsley, however, was smirking. Callie felt her blood start to boil. What had she been thinking? Heat or no, Aynsley was still a bitch.

"What's so funny?" Callie barked.

"The three of you," Aynsley replied breezily. "So completely intimidated by Isa."

"She does have the power to make or break your career," Ava pointed out.

"And to fire you," Callie finished.

"She's not going to fire you," Aynsley said with an exasperated sigh. Callie would've throttled her had she not been so desperate to know how Aynsley knew her job was secure.

"What makes you so sure?" Callie demanded.

Aynsley rolled her eyes. "Who fires interns? We're free labor. And if Isabel was going to fire someone, *she* wouldn't do the honors. She'd make Kiki do it."

"You think?" Callie said, relief dissolving her anger.

"Really, Callie. You've been here for weeks now. Haven't you figured anything out? Just go find out what it is," Aynsley insisted. "I'm sure she's got an errand for you and her assistant was too busy to call."

Callie turned to Ava, who was getting ready to make her latest food delivery to the park. "I'm sure she's right," Ava said hopefully.

Callie's heart was beating in her throat as she waited outside Isabel's office. The assistant was there. She offered Callie a bottle of Fiji, which she declined even though she was parched. Her hands were shaking so badly, she'd probably spill designer water right down her chest.

"Callie, *chère*, come in," Isabel trilled, leading her into the inner sanctum. It was a huge office, two walls of windows letting in the most incredible views all the way downtown to the Statue of Liberty. On the wall behind Isabel's marble slab of a desk was a huge blow-up of Madonna from fifteen years ago with a little *XX Madge* scrawled on the bottom corner—Callie knew it was the cover of the first issue of *Couture* Isabel had edited. Isabel motioned Callie toward a pair of black leather Eames chairs.

"So," Isabel said, clapping her hands together. "I understand that you are a designer."

It didn't seem humanly possible for Callie's heart to beat any faster, but now it went into overdrive. "Yes," Callie said, trying to remember the little speech she'd prepared for this very moment. "I've been sewing since I could walk and I've got some really innovative ideas. I know I'm young, but I think I have a lot to offer *Couture*, and—"

"I heard something about some shoulder bags you made," Isabel interrupted. "Like Stefani's L.A.M.B.

line, but more sophisticated, I'm told."

"I design lots of bags."

"These have faces on them."

"Oh, the silk screens?"

"*Oui*. Can you bring them in for me to see tomorrow?" Isabel asked.

"I'd be happy to, but I actually, *um*, have two here," Callie offered.

"*Parfait*. Go get them for me, and I'll call Marceline into my office."

"Now?" Callie asked, unsure if she was getting all this right.

Isabel glanced at her diamond-and-ruby-encrusted Rolex. "I have to go check up on the shoots now and to a dinner honoring Galliano after. *Ohh là là*, in this heat. But I have ten minutes, so *tout de suite*."

Callie rushed back to her office, and without a word to Nadine or Aynsley, she grabbed the bags as well as a portfolio of her designs and sketches that she'd been keeping in her desk drawer, just in case.

Marceline, the accessories editor, was already occupying the other Eames chair, looking bored and annoyed. Isabel was on the phone. She motioned for Callie to show the bags to Marceline. Callie pulled out Marilyn and Billie Holiday. Marceline reached out for them, her eyes narrowing.

Callie had fashioned the silk screens into hobo-type totes. Then she'd roughed them up a bit with sandpaper, giving them a distressed look, with hand-dyed swatches of silk for the lining. She'd sewn mesh tassels on the sides of each bag and stenciled a single word on each one—Love, Fame, Death, Beauty—in a gothic print in the corner. The straps were going to be chain metal or mesh. She'd picked up a few samples in the Garment District and had planned to test them out tonight. Then she just had to sew in the zippers and she was done.

The style was rough-hewn, edgy, a far cry from Callie's earlier, daintier designs. It was like the grit and glamour of the city had rubbed off on Callie and revolutionized her aesthetic. She tried to explain this to Marceline.

"I just need to add the chain for the strap. I had to find something that would look chunky, without being uncomfortable on the shoulder. I think this is the best one," she added. "It looks heavy, but it's really light."

"Hmm," Marceline said. "It's interesting. This style of bag is getting familiar, but the material breathes new life. The silk screens really make them fresh."

"I know," Callie said, and was about to explain how

she'd found them when Isabel interrupted.

"See. That is what makes a true designer. The bag, Marceline is right, it's very now. Very chic. And the material is *magnifique*."

"How long have you been silk-screening?" Marceline asked.

"Uhh, I kinda just got into it."

"Do you have others?" Isabel asked.

"I brought you my portfolio. As you can see," Callie continued, "my range extends beyond accessories."

Marceline's eyes narrowed even further and Callie could tell she'd said the wrong thing. "But handbags are my big passion these days. I'm doing a line of fifteen of the silk screens and I have others—"

"What's your price point?" Marceline interrupted.

"Huh?"

"How much will you charge for the silk-screen bags wholesale?" Isabel clarified.

Callie had no idea. To be honest, all week she'd been so consumed with making them that she hadn't even thought about what she'd do with them once they were finished.

"Obviously, they will be very expensive because the silk-screen process cannot be mass produced," Marceline said. "Perhaps the way to go is to number the bags, like lithographs."

"Ultra limited edition. *Quelle Couture*," Isabel added. "Ohh, look at the time. I must be off."

"Can I hang on to one of these?" Marceline asked.

"Uh, sure," Callie stammered. "But they still need the straps and zippers."

"Just leave the chain. We can pin it on for now," Marceline suggested. "I'll take Marilyn, if you please."

"Okay," Callie said, handing over the bag.

"I'm really impressed, Callie," Marceline said. "It takes vision to take a tired design and a famous face and come out with a fresh, even iconic, piece of fashion."

Callie replayed Marceline's words in her head over and over that afternoon, and for the next several days. She was right. It did take vision. Those silk screens had been festering in a box until she'd gotten hold of them. *She*, not the Brooklyn artist she'd bought them from, was the one who'd seen their potential. She'd transformed them into something new, something unique. So what if she let Marceline and Isabel believe that she'd made the fabric? The purses were her design, her *vision*. She created them, and that made them hers.

11

Two Scoops of Chocolate

NADINE COULD HEAR the sound of thunder growling outside. She envisioned the coming storm, and a bolt of lightning landing right on Kiki's head. That probably wasn't gonna happen. Oh well, at least the rain would sweep away the heat wave.

This whole damn day had been one giant pain in the ass. It was bad enough that Nadine was suddenly Kiki's whipping girl, but then Callie, who she was trying to be nice to—no easy feat with Sly vibrating bitchiness—had pranced back from her meeting, minus one of her bags and plus a shit-eating grin on her face. Callie kept sneaking Nadine these meaningful glances, begging

Ask me! Not a chance. It didn't take a genius to figure out what had gone down with Isabel, but no way was Nadine gonna give the girl a chance to gloat. Not today, anyhow. What pissed her off wasn't so much that Callie's bags had been noticed. They were smokin' cool. Nadine had been complimenting them all week, angling for one of the finished products. It was more Callie's drive, spending all night at that sewing machine of hers, doing her thing. Nadine was unpleasantly reminded that she was here to conquer New York, but that so far she hadn't conquered anything beyond a few bartenders and bouncers. She'd resolved to be more creative, and she'd been walking around the city taking pictures each day after work for the last week.

Ava returned from her latest errand just as the raindrops started to come down. "Woo, it is an oven out there," she said. "I saw Kiki, and she said the shoots are all done, so we can all blow out of here at five thirty."

"Great," Callie squealed. "We can celebrate!"

"Celebrate what?" Ava asked innocently. Nadine shot Aynsley a barely perceptible eye roll.

As Callie gushed about her fashion coup, and Ava listened like the nice girl that she was, Nadine glanced at her computer's clock: five fifteen. Fifteen minutes to freedom. Since there was no point shooting photos in a storm, there was only one way to end a day like this one. "I need a drink," Nadine announced.

"I'm always up for a cocktail," Aynsley said.

"Me, too," Callie piped up, rather brazenly inviting herself along. "I want to party," she said, looking so genuinely excited that for a second Nadine forgot to be aggravated.

"I guess we could do a group thing," Nadine offered. "How about you, Miss Straight and Narrow?" she asked, smirking at Ava. "Can you go out on a school night?"

Ava smiled broadly, her dimples popping with full force. "Sure, why not? We can be the Four Musketeers or something? What are there four of?"

"The four Horsemen of the Apocalypse," Aynsley suggested, grinning wickedly.

"I dig that," Nadine said, laughing.

"Me, too," Callie added.

"So where are we going?" Ava asked, looking at Aynsley.

"What am I? Social Coordinator?"

"Uh-huh. You *do* live here, Sly. And it doesn't hurt that you're on a first-name basis with every bouncer in Manhattan," Nadine replied.

Aynsley narrowed her eyes, and then started to

laugh. "You've got a point, Van Buren. We'll do the Fire Opal Bar by Gramercy Park. I'm on the permanent list there."

Two hours later they were sitting under a giant, multicolored Warhol painting—one of many at the candlelit bar-cum-gallery. Nadine had quite a precocious buzz going for such an early hour. She couldn't help herself. The bar made a delicious apple martini—or four of them in Nadine's case—and if anyone deserved to get drunk tonight, it was Nadine. Aynsley wasn't far behind, making quick work of a bottle of champagne. Callie and Ava were nursing glasses of sangria and munching on the platter of bar snacks that Aynsley had ordered and then ignored.

"I love the paintings in here," Aynsley said. "Did you see the Schnabel? He designed the bar, too."

"I'm a fan of the Bashquiat," Nadine said.

"It's Basquiat," Aynsley corrected.

"Not when you're as wasted as I am," Nadine whooped. "Hey, cute waiter dude. I. Need. Another."

"Maybe you should slow it down," Aynsley said. "It *is*, as you said, a school night."

"All the more reason to tie one on," Nadine said. "Drink myself into tomorrow. Kiki won't hurt so much if I've got a buzz on."

"Come on, Nadine," Ava said gently. "It's not that bad. Everyone gets grunt work." To which Callie, Aynsley, and Nadine all guffawed. *"What?"* Ava asked.

"Honey, you're the golden child," Nadine said. "You've never had to do a single Starbucks run. And now Callie is Isabel's new pet, and Sly here saved Kiki's ass in the LuxeLife meeting that *I* ruined, so all of you are superstars. Which is so wrong. *I* should be the superstar. Waiter," Nadine bellowed. "I need more booze."

"Speaking of Callie's big score," Aynsley began, her lips spreading into that Cheshire cat grin of hers. "Where did you learn to silk-screen, Cal?"

"Um, at school," Callie responded.

"I see," Aynsley replied. "Does—what was it?—Bexley Prep have a strong arts program?"

"Very," Callie said. "They pay a lot of attention to the whole liberal arts thing."

"Liberal arts means literature and history," Aynsley said, eyeing Callie.

Nadine thought she saw Callie blush in the dim glow of the candlelit bar. "I know that," she said quickly. "I meant that all of the arts are important."

"So do you have studio hours?" Aynsley pressed on.

"Something like that," Callie said. "I've got to hit the ladies' room. *Ava?*"

"Sure," Ava quickly agreed. "This sangria is running right through me."

As Callie and Ava went to the restroom, Nadine turned to Aynsley. "Sly?"

"Yes, Van Buren."

"You're a bitch, but that's okay, so long as you're *my* bitch."

"Right back at you. So can we ditch the good girls now? Jules keeps texting me. He's organizing a little soirée chez Rothwell. This place is dead."

"You got anything left in your liquor cabinet?" Nadine inquired. "I thought we cleaned it out a few nights ago."

"The Rothwell bar is stocked," Aynsley replied.

Ava and Callie returned from the bathroom, faces flush with freshly applied makeup. "I think we're going to call it a night," Callie said.

"This was so much fun, you guys. Thanks. And here," Ava said, laying down a pair of twenties, which Aynsley immediately waved off. Nadine had to hand it to Sly. Even at her cattiest, she was generous. Then again, she was spending someone else's money.

Once Ava and Callie had left, Nadine downed her martini, and Aynsley tossed back the last of the Perrier-Jouët. They got up to leave.

"Forgetting something?" Aynsley asked.

"Nah, I finished my drink."

Aynsley held up Nadine's black leather Canon bag and smirked. "Good to know you've got your priorities straight," she said with a smirk.

A quick car ride uptown and they were in front of the Rothwells' brownstone. The parlor-floor lights were blazing and music was thumping all the way to the street. Aynsley shook her head and smiled ruefully. "Jules, the golden boy. He could trash the house and Gregory and Cecelia would still think his Dean's List shit smelled like roses."

"Can't fault the boy for knowing how to throw a party, though," Nadine said.

When they reached the imposing oak front door, Julian swung it open. "Ladies," he said. "So nice of you to grace us with a visit." He looked at Nadine. "Sly mentioned you were in need of some candy-apple alcoholic deliciousness, so may I offer you one of these," he said, proffering a neon green martini. He handed Aynsley a goblet of red wine.

"Hmm, tasty," Nadine said, referring both to the drink and to Julian, who was looking extra fine tonight, all tanned and muscled in a pair of well-worn

Abercrombie chinos and an old surfer T-shirt. She loved the whole preppy-goes-beach-bum look.

Inside, about a dozen of the Rothwells' socialite pals, each of them identical in their meticulously casual clothes and their practiced blasé attitudes, were splayed out on the floral couches. Everyone was discussing who was summering where, and who was invited to the Lauder party. *Yawn*. No wonder Aynsley liked to party with Nadine. These people were so damn boring. Nadine sat down and promptly sucked back a second apple martini, waiting for the real festivities to begin.

One drink later, the party was still annoyingly sophisticated and staid. Nadine had had enough. "Let's get this joint going," she yelled, racing toward the stereo. She pulled off the Billie Holiday CD—no offense to Lady Day—and put on her favorite Nelly Furtado single. "Me and my girl Nelly are going to rock this house," she shouted as the first strains of "Promiscuous" pumped over the stereo. "Who's gonna sing with me? Who's gonna be my Timbaland?"

When there were no takers, Nadine jumped up on the beveled glass coffee table and started doing both parts: "'If ya lookin' for a girl that'll treat you right. If ya lookin' for her in the daytime with the light,'" she intoned. When it came to the chorus, Julian jumped up next to her, and sang Timbaland's part, "'Promiscuous, girl,'" he sang with a smirk almost identical to his little sister's. Nadine sang right back and at the end of the song whipped off her halter top, revealing a neon orange strapless push-up bra.

"Two scoops of chocolate right here," Nadine yelled, jiggling her chest.

"Okay, that's enough," Aynsley said, yanking Nadine down from the table. Nadine looked around and saw a roomful of shocked sneers, and for the strangest second thought she might cry. But then she looked at Aynsley's bemused and affectionate expression, and the feeling passed.

"Put this on," Julian said, throwing a seersucker blazer over Nadine's shoulders.

"Thanks. That was fun . . . but . . . *ohh*. Why is the room spinning?" Nadine asked. Julian and Aynsley led her over to a green damask couch, positively minimalist for Cecilia Rothwell's taste.

"Sly, get your friend some water," Julian ordered, as he sat down next to Nadine. Nadine collapsed into the cushions, her head toppling over onto Julian's lap. He was looking a little hazy around the edges. Hazy, but nice.

"Sly, your brother's a hottie," she called, though Sly

was currently in the kitchen. She looked into Julian's grape-green eyes. "You look just like that guy on *Entourage*. Vincent. Vinnie. Hey, Sly, your brother's Vinnie. That makes you Johnny Drama. Hahahaha."

Nadine felt the lights in the room start to dim. She lay there in Julian's lap, humming the "Superhero" theme from *Entourage*. After a while, she felt Julian gently lay her head down on the pillow. Then it was Aynsley shaking her.

"Wha?" Nadine asked, wiping away the drop of drool dribbling down her chin.

She felt Aynsley's arms around her shoulders, lifting her off the couch. "Come on, you. Time for bed."

Nadine let herself be carried upstairs to the guest room that was starting to feel like her second home. The last thing she remembered thinking before she passed out cold was that her friend Aynsley was a hell of a lot stronger than she looked.

12

The Twenty-One-Year-Old Spinster

WHEN AVA AND Callie stepped out of the Fire Opal Bar onto Lexington Avenue, the summer storm had passed, leaving the city sparkly clean and fresh.

"Look at that, you can see the stars," Ava said, as the pair linked arms and loped down Lexington toward their NYU dorm. "Pretty unusual for the city."

Callie skipped ahead, giggling like a madwoman. Now that Ava thought about it, Callie had drunk about twice as much sangria as she had. "Look how pretty," Callie squealed, jumping onto the iron gate around Gramercy Park, a small tree-shrouded urban oasis. "Can we go in?" She pulled on the locked gate.

"'Fraid not," Ava answered. "Only the lucky people who live in the town houses and swank apartments around the park get keys, though I wouldn't be surprised if Aynsley has one. She seems to hold the keys to every other exclusive haunt in the city."

Callie grimaced. "Ugh. She's such a snob." Callie ran her hands along the iron gate. "Besides, one day, I'm gonna be this huge designer. And I'll have a house here. Or maybe a loft in Tribeca like Isabel. Or a town house facing Central Park."

"You'll be in good company. See that house there?" Ava asked, pointing to an ornate limestone. "That's Julia Roberts's New York pied-à-terre. And Kate Hudson's got a place nearby, too."

"How do you know so much about the city? We've been here the same amount of time, but it's like you've lived here."

"Oh, you know. I visited the city a lot as a kid," Ava said, sounding a little nostalgic for simpler times. "And the city is just close enough to Vassar for weekend getaways."

"Lucky. I feel like such a rube sometimes. I've got a lot of catching up to do," Callie said as she stealthily plucked a fat purple hydrangea from a window box. "Whaddya say we start right now? Let's hit another bar." Callie licked her lips as her smile turned into a mischievous grin. "Besides, I've got to make good on my promise to find you a guy."

Ava glanced at her Tag Heuer. It was only nine thirty. She could stay out a little bit later, as long as things didn't get too crazy. Tomorrow was a Friday, and she had an important appointment. "Okay."

"Yay," Callie yelped, clapping her hands and jumping up and down. This was the guileless side of her that Ava loved, the one that seemed so completely excited by the fabulosity of New York, the one that didn't try to put on airs or out-sneer Aynsley. Sometimes it was as if Callie were two people—the goofy one standing right here with a fistful of stolen flowers, and an eagle-eyed fashionista clawing her way to the top. Of course, Callie wasn't the only one with a split personality.

"Where do you want to go?" Ava asked.

"Somewhere divey, but fun. Somewhere we can meet people our age. That Fire Opal Bar was cool and all, but everyone there was either Eurotrash or a rich old man. I like my guys *young* and rich," Callie explained.

"Speaking of which, have you heard from Monsieur Rothwell?" Ava asked coyly.

"Yep. We've been doing the whole email flirtation thing. It's funny though, I've been so *obsessed* with making my bags that I haven't had much time to obsess over him. And naturally, that's only upped his interest." Callie threw her arms up in the air. "It's so much easier playing hard-to-get when you're not faking it. And that's your number-one lesson when it comes to guys, Ava. When you have a lot going on in your life, they smell it, and want you more. If you're totally desperate, they bolt in the opposite direction."

"Thanks, Dr. Love. I'll file that little tip away," Ava said, tapping her head. "So I'm thinking we'll go to Roots. It's on Saint Marks."

"The street with all the punk, pierced, and tattooed guys?" Callie asked, just a tad surprised.

"Yep."

"So you've got a thing for bad boys, do you?"

"No," Ava said, feeling herself blush. Truth was, she had no idea what kind of guy was right for her. At this point she'd settle for a single one who liked her back. "It's got cheap beer and a great jukebox," she explained.

"Sounds good to me. Especially without the heiress footing the bill," Callie said with a bitter giggle. "Well, at least she's good for something. That and having a hot brother."

"How is it that you can be so mean and so nice at the same time?" Ava asked. Her tone was light and joking, but somewhere deep down she actually wanted to know how Callie divided up the different sides of herself.

"Everyone's like that," Callie replied. "Except you. You're just too nice. You've got to toughen up if you want to make it in the world of fashion—and in love, come to think of it."

Roots was about as different from the Fire Opal Bar as you could get—warped wood floors and smoke-stained walls instead of Deco tiles and modern art. But the place was packed with young, hot guys drinking pitchers of beer and playing darts. Callie pushed her way between two guys in leather jackets and waved down the bartender.

"Two Coronas and two tequila shots," she said triumphantly.

"Got some ID?" the bartender asked gruffly. Callie looked panicked for a minute, but Ava reached into her wallet, pulled out her license, and handed it over.

"Let me see your picture," Callie demanded, grabbing the ID.

"Hey, give that back," Ava whined.

"Aw, don't be shy. You look cute with bangs," Callie trilled. "But how'd you manage to get a New York City address on here? I heard that can help you land a job in the city, right?"

"Right," Ava replied flatly. "A friend of the family let me use her address."

"Oh," Callie said. "That's cool. Now let's drink a shot and find you a guy." She handed Ava back her ID, accompanied by a shot glass brimming with tequila.

Ava smelled the acrid aroma. "I'm not so sure tequila and sangria are the best combination, Cal."

"Who cares? Ready? One, two, three!" Callie knocked back the shot. Ava, on the other hand, took a small sip, winced, and gently set the glass back on the bar, where Callie snatched it up and quickly downed it for her. "Ahhh. Yummy. Okay, then, let's get to work. What do you think of him?" Callie pointed to a guy with brown hair in a ponytail and tight jeans.

Ava shuddered.

"You're right," Callie admitted. "Long hair only looks good on indie-rocker types, like Jack White. What about that guy over there?" she asked, gesturing toward a cutie with brown wavy hair, wiry arms, and a blocky armband tattoo.

Hmm. Ava admired the way his hair curled around the nape of his neck. This one actually had some potential—at least he did until his girlfriend came back from the bathroom and planted a territorial kiss on his lips.

"This is hopeless," Ava cried. "I'm a twenty-one-year-old spinster. I just don't know how any of this works. I guess I don't have the flirt gene in me like you do, Callie. *Callie?*" Ava was suddenly talking to the air. She scanned the dim room and spotted her friend's long mane of tawny hair making a beeline for the bar, turning heads as she went. Ava had no desire to be the frumpy girl in her wake, so she waited where she was, her beer growing sweaty and warm in her hands. After five minutes, Callie hadn't returned, so Ava pushed her way through the rocker types and found Callie. She was chatting up an absolutely adorable guy with floppy blond hair and a warm, open smile. Leave it to Callie to snag the cutest guy in the room.

When Callie spotted her, she started waving her hands wildly for Ava to join them. Ava slunk over, not thrilled to be a third wheel again. "See, isn't she just as pretty as I was saying? And she is unbelievably smart. One day she's gonna run *Couture*. And I'm gonna be the hot designer who knew her when."

Oh my god. Callie had obviously been talking her up to this guy. Ava was about to make excuses and bolt to the bathroom when the blond guy said, "Then it's a good thing I'm meeting you both, so I'll have double

I-knew-them-when bragging rights."

Ava couldn't help but smile, and the guy smiled, too. "I'm Reese," he said, offering her his hand. "Reese Kimble. Fashion ignoramus."

"Ava Barton," Ava replied shyly.

"Reese works for a film company. He's a producer," Callie explained.

"Actually, I'm a production assistant, but thank you for the promotion."

Ava couldn't help but giggle. He was cute *and* funny, and she detected a soft hint of an accent in his low voice. "Callie's ever the optimist," she said.

"I think José Cuervo is the real optimist here," Reese said, pointing to Callie, who was making quick work of another shot. Ava laughed again, and Reese joined in. Ava took the opportunity to peek at his blue eyes.

"I think you're probably right," Ava agreed. "You sound a little Southern." She ventured a guess. "Are you from Kentucky, by any chance?"

"You're close. Tennessee."

"I had a roommate from Kentucky in college, and she had a lilty accent like yours," Ava said, thankful that the room was dark enough to mask her now-crimson face.

"I'm from Memphis, but I'm impressed. You've got

a good ear. Two of them actually." Reese smiled shyly.

"Memphis! Like Elvis Memphis?" Callie asked, lurching forward in her high-heeled strappy sandals.

"Whoa there," Reese said, as he and Ava reached out to steady her.

"Have you been to Graceland?" Callie gushed. "To see Elvis? I mean, his stuff? He's dead, of course."

"I have been to Graceland, and I've even seen Elvis. In the flesh." Reese leaned in, adding in a conspiratorial whisper: "He's alive, you know." He sneaked an amused glance toward Ava. "I've seen him chowing on a chili cheese dog and a Slurpee at the Seven-Eleven in my hometown."

"You have not," Callie said, though she didn't look entirely convinced.

Reese waited a beat and then started chuckling. "Nah, but his face is still all over the city."

"That's so cool. You know I got—I mean, I made a silk screen of Elvis and turned it into a purse."

"I'm sure the King would be right proud to know he's a lady's handbag." Reese turned away from Callie and faced Ava. "So, Miss Barton, what do you do when you're not toiling away in the halls of fashion?"

"Oh, you know, this and that."

"This and that. Sounds scintillating."

"Well, *this* can be boring, but *that* is truly fascinating," Ava said, shocked to realize that she was actually flirting.

"How 'bout you show a Memphis boy how to properly do this and that in Manhattan?" Reese asked coyly.

Ava flushed with delight. "I could do that," she said, steadying her voice so she didn't sound too interested, just as Callie had instructed.

"Don't forget about the *this*," Reese teased. He reached into the back pocket of his skinny pegged trousers and pulled out a card from his well-worn leather wallet. "Here's all my info: work number, cell number, email address, website, social security. . . . Okay, maybe not that. But it lists all the ways to reach me, and shows you how obviously important I must be to have so many numbers. Anyway, call me, IM me, text me—you could even send a carrier pigeon."

Ava couldn't believe how adorable and funny this guy was. More than that, she couldn't believe that he wanted to go out with her. Things were going so well— she felt she had to get the hell out of here before she said something stupid to ruin it all.

"I will," she promised. "But Callie and I should probably go. We've got work in the morning, and I should start pumping her full of water so she doesn't feel too awful tomorrow."

"Sounds like a smart move," Reese said. "Good to meet you, Callie . . . and Ava." Reese winked at Ava, in a non-skeevy we're-partners-in-crime way, and Ava beamed as she steered Callie toward the door. She was smiling so hard she felt like her cheeks would crack.

"Nice dimples, by the way," Reese called out to her. Which only made Ava grin harder.

13
No Turning Back

DAMN, CALLIE, YOUR look is getting so hip," Nadine said. It was Monday morning and Nadine, Ava, and Callie were scanning their email and the phone messages that had piled up over the weekend. Aynsley, however, was absent. She was apparently taking a "mental health morning," at least that's how she'd put it in the voice mail she'd left, instructing the others to cover for her until noon.

"Thanks, Nadine. I made the pants over the weekend," Callie said, smoothing her charcoal gray low-slung linen menswear trousers. She'd matched them with a white ruffled silk Forever 21 blouse and a black button-up vest she'd borrowed off Ava. The look—sexy tomboy—was a new direction for her. Callie didn't know what it was—New York, *Couture*, or her trip to Williamsburg—but she felt her style evolving. And the funny thing was, though her new style was radically different from Callie's Ohio reality as the whole prep-school image she'd been trying to cultivate, her fashion transformation actually felt real, like it was coming from someplace deep down inside of her.

"You're gonna have to start dressing me soon," Nadine said.

"Soon, it'll be more than your bags that they notice around here," Ava insisted.

"I don't know about that. I've slipped three Callie Ryan originals into the fashion closet and haven't heard a thing back."

"You left your outfits in the closet?" Nadine asked admiringly. "Damn, I don't think even *I've* got that much chutzpah."

Callie doubted that, as she eyed Nadine's ensemble *du jour*: a Miss Sixty black-and-yellow-print dress with a plunging neckline that played up Nadine's, *err*, assets. Callie had seen the dress in magazines and knew that it went to the knee but Nadine had hemmed it thigh-high. She'd accessorized the dress with teetering black vinyl platforms, her blonde Afro wig, and sparkly gold eye shadow. She looked gorgeously outlandish, a total contrast next to Ava, who was the picture of East Coast restraint in a black-and-white starfish skirt with a red-checked Dana Buchman tank top that Callie had helped her pick out.

Kiki poked her head in. "Can you girls come into the conference room?" she asked, her eyes scanning the office. "Where's Aynsley?"

"I asked her to stop by the library for me," Ava replied. "To do a bit of background searching on accessory trends."

Kiki looked momentarily dubious, but then she shrugged. "Fine, then. You three. Chop, chop. Much to be done."

The girls filed into the conference room, where Marceline and Dieter were waiting. In the middle of the table was Callie's Marilyn bag. Everyone looked so serious, Callie feared that they'd found out about the silk screens. She was so busy conjuring excuses, she barely heard Kiki when she trilled "Congratulations."

Ava and Nadine both hugged her. "Huh?" Callie asked.

"Your bag is going to be featured in our October issue," Kiki repeated. "We're doing a whole spread on icons and fashion, and your bags are a perfect fit."

"Wow! I mean, *holy shit*. You mean, the bags I made are going to be in *Couture*?"

"Yes, Callie," Dieter said with a bitter little smile. "Isabel insisted on it." He looked less than thrilled with the idea. Then again, he'd pushed for the disastrous houndstooth story, so what did he know?

"When does the October issue hit stands again?" Callie asked. It never failed to confuse her how magazines all came out a month early, September arriving some time in August.

"The on-sale date is September tenth," Kiki replied.

Okay. That gave Callie two whole months to square things away with the silk-screen guy. She figured she could offer him a cut of the proceeds. Or maybe he wouldn't care. After all, when you buy material from someone you don't owe them a credit. This was different, she knew . . . oh, *forget it*. She'd figure it out by September. She exhaled, allowing some jubilation to filter in. "Gosh. This is fantastic," she began. "I can't believe it. And you should see some of the other stuff I'm working on, like these trousers."

Dieter sniffed. Kiki looked confused. Marceline rolled her eyes. Ava grabbed Callie's hand and squeezed it hard. "Oh, Callie. This is just wonderful.

What a lucky break," she said, her eyes boring into Callie's. Callie got the message: *Quit while you're ahead.*

"Don't forget, you promised me one of those bags," Nadine reminded her.

"Ah, maybe you can't afford to be so generous, Callie," Marceline warned. "You only have fifteen in the works. And you'll want to do some more silk-screening to meet the demand."

"But I can't," Callie cried. "I mean, my equipment's in Ohio."

"Right," Ava pointed out, "but you'll be back home by the time this comes out, so you can do more."

"Oh, right," Callie said, forcing herself to push any worries to the back of her mind. She'd have plenty of time to sweat the details later. Hell, she could even learn to silk-screen by then.

Announcement made, Kiki proceeded to hand out this week's assignments—Ava was to do research on thefashionistablog.com. Everyone in the industry was talking about it. And, the fact that the Fashionista remained anonymous made it all the more buzz-worthy. Callie was back to toiling in the fashion closet, and Nadine, clearly *still* on the shit list, was stuck filing contracts.

After Kiki dismissed them, Callie made her way to

the fashion offices, bummed that she had no one else to share her good news with. The assistant fashion editors who she worked under wouldn't be too happy to hear that an intern had scored such a coup. She thought about calling her parents, but they were at work. And besides, she could just hear her mom: "Oh, honey, isn't that nice." *Nice?* She had no idea. But Callie knew someone who would get it. Feeling bold, she flipped open her cell and dialed Julian. After four rings, he picked up.

"Hey, it's Callie," she said breathlessly.

"Well, well, look who's finally resurfaced," Julian drawled on the other end of the line. He sounded sleepy, but glad to hear from her.

"I'm sorry. Things have been crazy around here," Callie explained.

"Is that why Sly just left for work? Because she's recovering from the craziness?"

"I don't know why *she's* crazed," Callie said. "But I've been busy designing handbags. And now they're going to be featured in the October *Couture*."

"You landed your designs in *Couture*?" Julian asked.

"I did," Callie said triumphantly.

"You work fast," he said with a laugh. "I've never heard of Isabel taking to someone new so quickly."

"I think they like the whole idea of discovering some rube teenager from Ohio," Callie joked.

Julian laughed. God, he sounded sexy. "I don't think anyone would mistake you for a rube," he said dryly.

"You know what I mean. Anyhow, I wanted to share the news—and apologize for being so out of touch."

"I suggest we celebrate the former and remedy the latter," Julian said. "I'm in the Hamptons today, but I'll be back tomorrow morning. How about we do lunch in the park?"

"I'd love to," Callie trilled.

Callie floated the rest of the day, with her twin victories— first the bag, then Julian—competing for her delight. Not even Aynsley, who was horribly late and refused to acknowledge Callie's good news, could pop Callie's balloon.

The next day she dressed carefully in the Anna Sui orange silk dress with paisley print trim that she'd picked up at INA, a high-end consignment shop in Nolita that she'd read about in the Fashionista blog. She piled her hair on top of her head, leaving strands to fall in suggestive tendrils across her tan shoulders. She wore an onyx necklace, the pendant part dipping way into her cleavage. It was the perfect look—edgier and sexier than your typical society girl.

The morning inched by, hour by hour, but finally it was twelve thirty. She'd arranged to meet Julian at the statue in front of the Columbus Circle entrance to the park. Kiki had given her the okay to take a long lunch, so long as she kept her cell phone on.

Callie purposely arrived a little bit late. If she'd learned one thing from Aynsley, it was that socialites seemed to regard punctuality as a character flaw. As she was crossing the traffic circle at twelve forty-five, she saw Julian walk up to the statue. Perfect. So long as he was there first. She appraised him from a distance. He looked like he'd just bounced in off the beach, wearing tan drawstring pants, a white linen shirt, and brown suede flip-flops. In one hand he carried a blue blanket, in the other a big canvas bag with a monogrammed JR on it.

"Well, well, if it isn't the hottest new designer in town," Julian said, grinning at Callie as she approached.

"I bet you say that to all the girls," Callie said, flashing a coquettish grin.

"Only the really pretty ones who can sew," he said, leaning over and kissing Callie lightly on the mouth.

Callie breathed in the scrumptious aroma coming from Julian's bag and sighed. *"You cooked?"*

"I shopped. At Balducci's. I thought we'd do it Continental-style. Lots of salads and cheeses. And some prosecco," he said, pulling out a bottle of Italian bubbly. He took her hand and led her through the park until they reached the Sheep Meadow. Then he spread out a blanket and revealed a stunning array of food. "Uh-oh. Looks like I forgot forks," he said sheepishly.

"You'll have to feed me then," Callie replied.

"Then my master plan is succeeding," Julian said, his blue-green eyes glinting.

Using their fingers, Julian and Callie ate artichoke salad, duck liver pâté, Gruyère cheese, mushroom risotto, heirloom tomatoes in balsamic vinegar, and crispy, still-warm French baguette. Callie didn't know what half of the stuff was, but she pretended everything was as familiar as a peanut butter and jelly sandwich. It was all delicious. And having Julian feed her bits of it, well that was an entirely different kind of tasty. After they'd eaten and polished off the bubbly, he pulled out four huge chocolate-covered strawberries.

"I'm afraid these melted a bit," he said.

Callie bit into one, the juice of the berry dripping down her face, the chocolate smearing her hands.

"Let me help you with that," Julian said, taking Callie's fingers and sucking off the chocolate. "Oh, I think you've got some right there." He pointed to Callie's face.

"Here?" she asked, pointing to her cheek.

"More like here," he said, touching the corner of Callie's lips. "I'd better clean that off before it stains your pretty dress." He leaned in and kissed her. Callie opened her mouth to kiss him back, tasting the chocolate still on both of their lips. Callie moved closer as Julian pressed his body into hers. She ran her hands under his shirt, feeling the smooth muscles of his chest. Julian's fingers were working their way down the front of her necklace, feeling for the pendant, and sending a delicious shiver up her spine.

"You are so hot," he murmured as he nibbled on her ear. "Why the hell are we in the middle of the park?"

"No one's looking," Callie said, nibbling on his neck. She grabbed the drawstring of his pants and twirled it in her hands. Julian cocked his head to one side in surprise and Callie grinned. She pulled him closer. "On second thought, maybe we should sneak into the woods," she suggested.

"Hmm, I'm with you," Julian said. "Hey, what's vibrating? I think your phone is ringing," he said, shifting over and removing Callie's turquoise ruched silk clutch from under his leg. "Felt good, though."

Callie grabbed the phone and glanced at the caller ID. Damn, it was from *Couture*. "Hello," she said, mouthing a "Sorry" to Julian.

"Callie, it's Kiki. We're having a bit of an emergency and we need you back in the office."

"Now?" Callie asked.

"Preferably five minutes ago. Get in a cab and come straight to my office."

"Oh, shit," Callie said, snapping her phone shut.

"Picnic *interruptus*," Julian said with a smirk.

"I'll bet it's nothing." Callie groaned. "They probably just need another bag packed for a shoot next week or something. I'm so sorry."

"Don't worry about it." Julian grinned. "I'll be fine."

"Really?"

"After my cold shower," he said with a leer. "We'll get together soon. I'm hopping over the pond for a while, but I'll be back a week from Monday."

"Oh," Callie said, trying to hide her disappointment. She wondered how many girls he'd be picnicking with in Europe. Julian walked her to Central Park West, hailed her a cab, and gave her a peck on the lips before she drove away.

It was hot. Callie was hot. In need of a cold shower herself. And in no mood to be bossed around by the bitchy fashion closet girls. She trudged into Kiki's office, where Marceline, Isabel, and Dieter were gathered. Callie felt a familiar sense of panic creep back. She'd been found out.

"Here's our savior," Isabel trilled as Callie entered the room.

"Huh?" Callie asked, utterly perplexed.

"Big crisis, Callie," Kiki explained. "We just found out that Eamon Sinds is being featured in a huge spread in *Style*'s next issue."

Callie recognized Eamon Sinds as the English handbag maker who Aynsley was all tight with. What this had to do with her, she couldn't begin to say.

"*Couture* was going to feature Sinds as our hot new handbag designer in the Cutting Edge Designers Showcase," Isabel explained. "And we've essentially been scooped by *Style*. Pfft. What a joke! *Style* doesn't have a stylish page in its pathetic little spine. How did they manage Sinds for a six-page feature? *Merde!*"

"But the good news for you," Kiki explained, "is that we're crashing your bag into our next issue. You're going to be our hot new handbag maker for the Cutting Edge feature. So you need to go finish the strap, glue it if you have to, because we're shooting it tomorrow. You'll be shot for the issue, too. And you'll come to the Cutting Edge Gala. I'm sure I don't have to tell you what a huge break this is."

Callie's head was spinning with booze, lust, ambition, and surprise. She walked out of Kiki's office to the intern room, where Ava, Nadine, and even Aynsley were waiting for her to celebrate. She could barely talk. Her bag was going to be in *Couture* as part of the Cutting Edge showcase. Not only was she going to be in the magazine itself, she was going to be a guest of honor at one of the hottest fashion events in town. Not in her wildest dreams had she imagined this kind of a trajectory. And yet, the silk-screen guy, his work was going to be in the magazine passed off as her own in less than three weeks. Callie had the sense that events were now totally out of her control. It was like fate had been leading her to this moment. There was no turning back now.

"I loathe narcissism, but I approve of vanity."

Filed under: Fashionista > Style

There goes the Fashionista again, reaching back in time to quote the fashion icons of yesteryear. This particular jewel was voiced by the incomparable editor in chief of all things stylish, Diana Vreeland. And I must say, I do agree with her wholeheartedly. Vanity, an admittedly superficial pride in one's appearance, is fine. It's a fashion must, really. If we girls weren't vain, then Zac Posen and Tom Ford would be woefully unemployed. Nor would there be any reason to splurge on Oscar de la Renta snakeskin sandals. Or shimmery Trish McEvoy cosmetics. Or Harry Winston jewels (divine!). It's vanity that drives the desire for prettiness, and the Fashionista has nothing but good things to say about prettiness. »

Narcissism, however, is another story. Yesterday, for example, the Fashionista had to endure a coterie of socialites engaged in a competitive name-dropping fest. The day before, I suffered through the self-important blatherings of some wannabe fashion designer. Then, at a <u>Marc Jacobs</u> sample sale, I had the pleasure of listening to a pair of Hollywood starlets crudely brag about the number of <u>A-list actors</u> they'd dated. They ranked their exes by box-office draw! Need I go on?

Vain girls are interesting—always chasing after some eye-catching new clutch or sparkly sandal. Narcissists, on the other hand, are a bore—blah-blah-blahing, and me-me-meing. Somebody, wake me when it's over!

Your faithful Fashionista

14

And the Academy Award for Best Poseur Goes to . . .

AYNSLEY DESERVED AN Academy Award. For the last several days, she'd been playing the part of Aynsley Rothwell, enthusiastic (well, enthusiastic-ish) co-intern to one Callie Ryan. Callie herself was about to be anointed the new It Girl handbag designer by *Couture* magazine, and so was about to be crowned the hottest new handbag designer by every slavish fashionista in the country. As Callie reveled in the spotlight, Aynsley went along with it: took the girls out for celebratory drinks at Le June, smiled when Callie announced that soon she'd be able to get into the hot clubs without Aynsley's help (the question was, would she be able to pay for her own drinks without the help of Gregory Rothwell's black Amex?). She'd handed over her cell phone when Jules had called from Europe so Callie could say "hi" and play cute as he congratulated her for the umpteenth time. Aynsley wished she could tell Jules to cut it out, stop feeding the flame, but that would run contrary to her little act.

The rationale for Aynsley's ruse was two-fold. For one thing, she knew that being snarky in the face of Callie's fashion score would look like sour grapes. And Aynsley was *not* jealous that Callie had gotten her bag in *Couture*. It was a cute bag. Nowhere on the level of a Sinds, but as far as Aynsley was concerned, he'd made his bed by reneging on his exclusive with *Couture* to whore himself out to that second-rate rag, *Style*. Had it been Nadine or even Ava whose bag was about to become the must-have accessory, Aynsley herself would've been bragging to all her friends that she had the inside track on the next great trend.

The problem wasn't Callie's success. It was Callie herself. Aynsley knew she wasn't the only one acting, because Callie was up to some Oscar-worthy fakery of her own. If there were an Academy Award for poseur, it would go to . . . Country Callie Ryan. Aynsley knew this with as much certainty as she knew that wedge

heels were on the verge of over—Callie was a fraud.
Sure, some things about her were legit. The girl could
sew. And obviously, she could get a boy's attention—
Jules had called her every day from Antibes. But there
was something about Callie that was blatantly fake, and
Aynsley had decided that she was going to find out
exactly what it was. And because, as Cecilia always
liked to say, you can catch more flies with honey,
Aynsley Rothwell was now playing the part of supportive gal pal.

"What's today's torture?" Aynsley asked. It was
Friday morning, and she'd breezed in late for the third
time this week. She knew it was dangerous, but she also
figured she had a little currency left from the LuxeLife
incident.

"Why, Sly. How nice of you to grace us with your
presence," Nadine said with that ballsy grin of hers. She
was looking as *Nadine* as ever in an über-tight black
gingham dress, paired with a black straw cowboy hat
(complete with red feather) and fluffy red mules.
Aynsley, on the other hand, was as low-key casual as
her friend was outré. She had on a pair of Rag & Bone
skinny jeans and a lilac Marc Jacobs top with ruffles
down the front, and a cute little tie that made the whole
thing feel professional. Her silk lilac Prada slides were

the perfect finishing touch.

"I aim to please," Aynsley said. "Nice outfit."

"Thanks. It's my ghetto cowgirl look," Nadine said proudly.

Ava laughed. "You should patent that."

"Good thing you showed," Callie said. "Kiki just announced an important meeting with our publicist. Something about the Cutting Edge Gala."

Aynsley had to literally force her eyes wide open to keep from rolling them. It was as if Callie was incapable of speaking without gloating. All week, they'd been hearing Callie muse about the gala: Who would be there? What would she wear? Aynsley took a deep breath and turned to Nadine. "What publicist?"

"Party planner for this big shindig. Lucy Nelson or something."

"Lucy Gelson," Aynsley corrected. "The party planner/publicist extraordinaire. My mother's worked with her on charity galas. She's a total bitch."

"I can't wait to hear about this party," Callie said. "I can't wait to *go* to this party!"

"Funny that you'll be the help and a guest at the same time," Aynsley jabbed. She couldn't help herself. The cut flew right over Callie's head anyhow.

"We better go," Callie said, standing up and stretching. She was wearing a pair of low-slung white shorts and the white halter she'd made a while ago. A black leather braided belt cinched in her tiny waist. It was a chic outfit. Aynsley had noticed that Callie's style was getting more sophisticated, a shift that she greeted with equal parts relief (seeing someone ill-outfitted physically pained her) and annoyance (score another point for The Faker). Aynsley also noticed that now that Callie was toning down her look, Ava had taken to wearing her buddy's castoffs. Today, for instance, she had on Callie's turquoise skirt with the cutaways. The funny thing was, a skirt that had looked garish on Callie actually gave Ava's plain-Jane look a necessary boost.

They filed into the conference room, where Kiki was sitting head-to-head with the renowned publicist Lucy Gelson. With her platinum blond hair, pouty lips (courtesy of monthly collagen injections), and her midriff-baring ensembles, from a distance Lucy looked like she was in her twenties. But a close-up look, behind her Gucci wrap-around shades and piles of Chanel foundation, revealed a woman almost as old as Aynsley's mother. "Mutton disguised as lamb," that's how Julian had described Lucy after she'd attempted to seduce him at Diddy's White Party in the Hamptons two summers ago. Naturally, Julian had refused. He did have *some* standards.

Kiki and Lucy looked up as the girls sat down. Kiki whispered something into Lucy's ear and then she and her lizard Jimmy Choos clicked out of the conference room. Lucy, looking vampy in a strapless Versace minidress with a peek-a-boo slit just above the boobs, sighed as though the mere sight of the girls exhausted her.

"Ladies. Aynsley," she welcomed them.

"Hi," the girls responded in unison.

Lucy waved her arms in the air as if about to conduct an orchestra. "Aside from Fashion Week, this is *the* event of the year. And most certainly the party of the year. So it has to be perfect. Seamless." She eyed the girls suspiciously, as though she doubted they had the stuff. So condescending. Even more so, knowing, as Aynsley knew, that Lucy Gelson was a college dropout, who'd gotten into the PR business when her husband left her for another man. She'd managed to cover up the scandal so thoroughly that the jet set had crowned her a master of spin.

"This year. We have the ultimate venue. The Apple Store in Soho. It is itself a cutting-edge architectural space, and since Apple, of course, represents cutting-edge technology, it creates a perfect metaphor. I'll have pros coming in to style the place, but I'll need you girls to liaise with the caterer and help with the guest list. *Ava*," she said, staring at Callie.

"I'm over here. That's Callie," Ava called.

"Callie, I'll need to talk to you later. We've got to make sure your look at this party is beyond reproach." She turned to Ava. "Ava. I'm told you're the responsible one, so I need you to take charge with the caterers. I have an appointment set up for this afternoon."

"Oh. I'm so sorry," Ava stammered. "I have a doctor's appointment today."

Lucy frowned. Nadine and Aynsley exchanged a look. This was Ava's third appointment in as many weeks. Either Ava was getting Botox treatments or she was seriously sick. Then again, she could be going to a shrink. In which case, why hide it? Everyone who was anyone was in therapy.

"But Nadine can do it," Ava added.

"From what I hear, Nadine's on the bench," Lucy spat. "So she'll just be assisting the rest of you."

Aynsley looked at Nadine, willing her to keep her mouth shut. Lucy Gelson was a powerful woman, and there was no point pissing her off. Nadine looked indignant but kept her lips sealed for once.

"Nadine has fantastic organizational skills, and she's written quite a bit about the Philadelphia culinary scene. It's really hot, as you know," Ava added. Of course Lucy wouldn't know, Aynsley thought. The woman didn't leave the greater Manhattan area unless it was to go to the Hamptons, South Beach, or Beverly Hills.

"I'll oversee her, make sure everything runs smoothly," Ava promised.

Lucy waved her hands in the air again. "Fine. Nancy, you're on catering detail."

"It's Nadine," Nadine said, but sheepishly. The girl was learning.

"Well, whatever your name is, don't blow it. This is a big responsibility. You'll need to meet with the caterers several times over the next two weeks."

"No prob," Nadine replied, with only the tiniest trace of 'tude.

"Aynsley, I'd like you to help with the guest list. Obviously, invites to all the must-have people, fashion luminaries, models, this year's honorees, etc. went out weeks ago. But we'd like to court some young blood. Your set. Just invite everyone who's invited you to a party in the last few years. I want the velvet ropes to be thronged. You know how this works."

"Of course I do, Lucy," Aynsley said. "I'll make sure this is the event of the year."

"No, *I'll* make sure of that," Lucy insisted. "This is going to be the only soirée people come back to the city for in July. You make sure the guest list is hot. And Callie, you can help out. Have Aynsley tutor you. She can tell you who's who in this world you're about to join." Lucy smiled, or attempted to with her puffer-fish lips. "Oh, yes. We're going to hang these fabulous blowouts of the magazine spreads on the wall, with each designer's photo. And we'll run a brief but quirky bio on each one. Aynsley, since you already have personal relationships with half of these fashion people, Kiki thought you'd be a natural to do the reporting. Which means you'll be interviewing Callie here."

Callie beamed, and Aynsley grinned along with her. And it wasn't even a fake grin. Interviewing Callie was like a gift delivered on a silver Tiffany platter. It gave her a license to probe, and she had the feeling that, as devious as Callie was, she herself was ten times so. She'd crack this country girl for sure.

"All right, then," Lucy said, snapping her brown-and-orange ostrich Hermès Birkin bag shut. "I'll expect daily progress reports from each of you. We have exactly two weeks to pull this thing off, and I've got three other parties going," she added, "so I'm relying on you girls not to muck this up. If you do, I'll skin you alive." Lucy winked, as if to show she was kidding, but the effect on her Botox-paralyzed face was more than a tad chilling.

The interns filed out of the conference room with assurances that they'd knock this out of the park. They were buzzing with excitement about the glamorous project. Even Aynsley, who found Lucy's condescension vaguely insulting, was too pleased with the prospect of a Callie interrogation not to smile.

"So, when do you want to do the interview?" Callie asked with a huge grin. She could hardly keep from jumping up and down. Clearly, she was clueless.

"We'll figure it out," Aynsley said casually. She had to get Callie at the perfectly vulnerable moment.

"I'll see you guys later. I'm off to the doctor's," Ava said. "I wish I could stick around." She looked genuinely pained.

"Hey, Ava, thanks for your help getting me off of shit patrol around here. That was a selfless move," Nadine said.

Ava smiled, her whole face transformed from distracted to delighted. "You're welcome. I think they overdid your punishment, by the way. I mean, you did, after all, fry your hair. Anyhow, I'll see you all later."

After Ava left, Nadine turned to Callie. "Do you know why she goes to the doctor so much?"

"She doesn't go that much," Callie said.

"Are you serious?" Nadine retorted. "She's always cutting out for an appointment here or there."

Callie frowned. "I'm sure it's nothing. She seems perfectly fine."

"I hope so," Aynsley said, and she meant it. She actually liked Miss Goody Two Shoes, even if she was BFF with Country Callie.

"Me too," Nadine agreed. "But, I should run to the caterer's office." She thumbed through the sheaf of papers Lucy had given her. "It's Clayton something or other, right?"

"Clayton Company. They did Mother's last two affairs," Aynsley said. "Very organic, Alice Waters disciples, all the rage right now."

"I hope they've got some samples. I'm starving. And a little hung over still," Nadine admitted.

"What else is new, Van Buren?" Aynsley laughed. She couldn't remember the last time her friend *hadn't* been hung over.

"I'm nothing if not dependable," Nadine said. She grabbed her red vinyl tote bag and headed for the elevators.

"Want to do the interview now, Aynsley?" Callie asked eagerly. Her hazel eyes were shining with excitement.

"Not now," Aynsley replied flatly. "We need to get to work convincing the Who's Who of Manhattan to clear their schedules for gala night." Aynsley smiled, resuming her Academy Award–winning performance of Supportive Gal Pal.

15

As Tasty As a Philly Cheesesteak

NADINE FELT LIKE she had just staged a prison breakout as she passed through the security turnstiles and into Conrad Publishing's crowded lobby that Friday morning. Finally, someone—Lucy Gelson of all people—had loosened her leash, allowing her to travel farther than the nearest Starbucks. She strode out of the building, inhaling the muggy stink of 42nd Street before jumping into a cab—they always stopped for her, but it never hurt to show a little leg.

As the cab crawled through Friday-afternoon tunnel traffic toward the caterer's office, Nadine perused the Clayton Company files that the publicist chick had given her. Aynsley had been kind when she described Lucy. After meeting her, though, Nadine knew without a doubt that the woman was *beyond* a bitch. She'd dissed Nadine like she was some know-nothing moron. And she wasn't the only one. Lately everyone at *Couture* had been treating Nadine like the resident whipping girl. Not that the staffers had ever been bastions of warmth. They *were* fashion people, after all. Nadine wasn't naïve enough to expect the fashionistas to kiss her ass. But, in the beginning at least, they'd admired her style—which was wilder than that of any of the skinny chicks that buzzed through the mag's hallways. In fact, Kiki used to chuckle at Nadine's getups, referring to her as "*Couture*'s own Beyoncette." But now? Forget it. If people weren't staring right through her as though she were invisible, they were recoiling as if she had a funky smell to her. It was enough to get a girl paranoid. Nadine had taken to doubling up on deodorant and chewing more gum, just to be on the safe side.

When her mom called to check up on things, Nadine kept up a brave front and told her all kinds of lies about the fantastic assignments she was doing. Didi Van Buren would be none too pleased to learn that Nadine was spending what was supposed to be her career-making summer working neither as a photo assistant nor as a fledgling reporter. She'd been toiling away as a gofer. Plus, if Nadine told her mom about the whole bottom-of-the-totem-pole treatment, she could just picture Didi getting all uppity and claiming that Nadine's mistreatment was a Black Thing. Which it wasn't. *Couture* had a multicultural staff—although all the colors of the rainbow were just as snooty as the white chicks.

Truth was, no way could Nadine tell her mom the whole story. That would mean mentioning the LuxeLife incident, which would require explaining that Nadine had fallen asleep with the product on, which might open the Pandora's Box of reasons why Nadine was so damn tired in the first place. Didi was a lot of things, but dumb wasn't one of them. She knew her daughter liked to party, and she'd warned her not to blow this once-in-a-lifetime shot by letting Manhattan's many diversions seduce her. Maybe things had gotten a little crazy these last few weeks, but if Sly could manage to toss back a bottle of Pinot, stumble to bed at two a.m., and still show up to work the next day pulling fashion miracles out of her ass, then Nadine was determined to do the same.

Nadine sighed and looked at her watch. Three o'clock. Three more hours till she and Sly could ditch

Couture for the weekend and Nadine could let loose. She wanted a drink. Or some food at least. She glanced at the catering menu, but it wasn't all that appealing: Thai tuna tartare (her stomach couldn't handle raw fish right now), trout caviar (ditto), chilled vegetable soup in a shot glass. (A shot? Yes. But not one full of cold cucumber soup.) Never mind all that bullshit Ava had said about Philly's culinary scene. What Nadine really craved was a cheesesteak sandwich, heavy on the Cheez Whiz. Fat chance of that, though. Nadine was convinced that New Yorkers subsisted on nothing but sushi, smoothies, and coffee.

The cab crawled down Ninth Avenue. At this rate, Nadine was gonna be late. Another black mark, another chance to get reamed out by Kiki or Lucy. Which seriously blew. *What?* Now Nadine was supposed to control the flow of traffic through the Lincoln Tunnel?

"Hey, my friend. Any way you can move faster?" Nadine asked her cabbie.

"Where you want me to go? Traffic is heavy all over. It's Friday, so everyone leaving the city," he replied, clearly suggesting that if Nadine were anyone, she'd be leaving, too.

"Just take a shortcut. Get us out of this mess."

"Whatever you say. You're the boss," the cabbie said

with a smirk, and then went back to yammering on his cell phone in some other language.

The driver went all the way over to the West Side Highway, where traffic was a smidgen better, but then he got completely lost among the twisting cobbled streets of the West Village.

"It's Ninth Avenue and Fourteenth Street. It's a major intersection. How hard is that to find?" Nadine exclaimed.

"You the one who wanted to take a detour," the cabbie reminded her.

"I know, I know," Nadine mumbled. Out of the corner of her eye she spotted a familiar red awning. Palais—it was the bistro they'd eaten at the first night of their internship. Cool. Maybe now Nadine could find their way out of the maze. She peered into the restaurant, trying to get her bearings, and did a double take. There, sitting out on the patio, was Ava's look-alike. Wait a second. Ava's doppelgänger was wearing Callie's turquoise skirt. And smiling with Ava's dimples. And sipping wine with a gray-haired hottie old enough to be her father. To judge their body language—their heads close together, Ava's eyes darting around, as though keeping an eye out for someone (the Silver Fox's wife, perhaps?)—it was pretty damn clear that they were up to something worth hiding.

Well, well, it sure explained all of Ava's furtive meetings, not to mention her weekly "doctor's" appointment (more like playing doctor, Nadine guessed). The Silver Fox *had* to be married. She could see the whole scene: Friday morning, Wifey slips away to Bridgehampton, and the old rascal plans a rendezvous with his young mistress. It was the perfect scheme. Hell, even the cabbies knew that everyone else ditched town on summer Fridays.

So Ava's whole I'm-a-virgin, not-up-on-the-sexy thing had been an act? Damn. Nadine had always prided herself on being able to read people, but Miss Ava Barton and her innocent routine had sure fooled her. It had fooled them all.

"Hold up a minute," Nadine told the cab driver. She wanted to get a better look at Ava and her sugar daddy. But the cabbie chose this moment to pound the gas. Within a second, they'd turned the corner and were on Hudson, just blocks from the caterer. Nadine grabbed her cell, ready to call Sly with this delicious morsel of gossip, but as her finger poised to hit speed dial, her conscience surfaced and she snapped the phone shut. What if she had the wrong idea? Ava really did seem like a nun in training. Could she actually be bedding a

George Clooney clone? A *married* George Clooney clone? She needed to get more info. Find out who Ava's Silver Fox was. Get a picture, maybe, and show it to Sly—she seemed to know half the people in town, and *all* of the rich ones, and this guy looked like money. Or maybe she should cut the undercover act altogether. Ava had seriously stepped up for her with Lucy this morning. The least Nadine could do was repay that courtesy with a little discretion.

So for now, Nadine would just have to keep her secret to herself. In fact, it made her feel better about her own lowly status at *Couture* to know that even the good girl had some dirt to hide.

The cab pulled up in front of Chelsea Market, home to Clayton Company. Nadine paid the driver and gave him a five-dollar tip. He looked a little surprised, but what he didn't know was that his little detour had given Nadine a satisfying reminder that she wasn't the lone screw-up. Everyone had their foibles and everyone put their foot in it now and again. That realization *plus* a juicy new piece of gossip to savor—well, let's just say, it was as tasty as a Philly cheesesteak.

"Thanks, lady," the cabbie called.

"No, thank *you*," Nadine replied as she made her way to the caterer's office.

16

Cinderella, Post-Fairy Godmother

CALLIE PULLED OFF her heels as soon as she got to the lobby of her dorm that Friday evening. Four weeks in New York and her feet looked like they belonged to a firewalker. The dorm was buzzing with summer-school students getting ready for the weekend. Callie wove through the unruly masses. When she'd arrived in New York, all the college students had seemed so much older than she was, but now, Callie felt like she had decades on them.

She made her way to the elevator. She sure hoped Ava was home. She'd declined an invite to hit the chi-chi happy hour circuit with Nadine and Aynsley. It had been nice of them to ask, but the prospect of a night with Aynsley (who, even at her nicest, still made Callie feel like some dorkball from the sticks), with no chance of seeing Julian—who was out of town until next week—well, thanks but no thanks. Ava hadn't mentioned leaving for her parents' house, but it had been such a crazy week with her bag being chosen and her all-too-short date with Julian, that she'd forgotten to ask if Ava had plans. When Callie got to Ava's dorm room and saw that the door was ajar, she was elated. Her weekend was saved. She rapped gently on the door and it nudged open enough to reveal Ava, who was pacing in the corner talking on her cell.

"Hi, honey, I'm home," Callie called, entering the bedroom.

Ava didn't look all that happy to see Callie. She frowned and flushed. "I gotta go," she whispered into the phone. "I'll talk to you later. Not tonight. I'll see you soon, okay? Sorry. I've got to go," Ava said insistently before snapping her cell shut. She turned to Callie. "Hey. Sorry. I didn't hear you knock."

"Who were you talking to?" Callie asked in a sing-songy voice. She had a strong feeling that Ava had been talking to a guy!

"No one you know," Ava replied.

"Now, that's not true, is it?" Callie teased.

"What?" Ava asked, with a note of embarrassment in her voice.

"Come on, you can tell me. After all, I'd do the same if I were you."

"Really?"

"Yeah. Only if that Reese hottie asked me to call him, I wouldn't have waited a whole week. I think you're taking the whole playing-hard-to-get thing too far."

Ava's face went crimson. Callie had her. "I knew it! I knew it! I could tell you guys would hit it off," Callie continued. "Are you going on a date? Are you going out with him tonight?"

"No," Ava replied, looking a little jittery.

Poor girl. She was so completely naïve when it came to guys. Look how undone she was after a single phone call.

"Well, that's good. At least we can hang out. I feel like doing something mellow. Catching a movie at the Angelika or something. But can I just say? Reese! Yay!" Callie squealed. "You guys are gonna fall in love and get married, and you'll have to let me be a bridesmaid. And of course, I'll design the dresses, yours and the maids' gowns. Oh my god. Look at your face.

You're totally horrified. I'm just kidding about the marriage thing, but I *so* had a feeling about you two. You should totally go out on a date already. Maybe we can double date when Julian gets back from France. We can all go to Brooklyn." Callie dropped her shoes and bag and flopped onto the white cotton duvet on Ava's twin bed.

"Do you like steak? We'll have to go to Peter Luger's. It looks like a total dive but they serve the most amazing food there. Or maybe we should go to Red Hook. I keep reading how that's the next hot area in Brooklyn. You know, Brooklyn's the new Manhattan, Manhattan's some mall in Jersey. Or something like that. Are you okay? You look a little green."

"I'm just a little tired," Ava groaned.

Callie suddenly remembered Ava's latest visit to the doctor and felt a pang of fear. "Was everything all right, you know, with the doctor?"

"Oh, it's fine," Ava replied absentmindedly.

"You're not sick or anything?" Callie blurted.

"I have allergies," Ava explained, looking a bit dazed.

"Well, I'm glad that's all it is," Callie said, relieved. "Hey, I'm parched. Do you have any water?"

"There's a bunch of Poland Spring in the fridge,"

Ava said, gesturing to the kitchenette. Callie padded toward the kitchen, but she was stopped in her tracks by a swath of pink netting peeking out from the closet. She opened the door. Inside was the most amazing frock: a tight-bodiced, tulle-skirted, periwinkle silk dress, overlaid with pink netting. Inside the netting, dozens of multicolored silk petals swam around. She pulled out the dress and checked the label. Alexander McQueen—no wonder it was so gorgeous. But his stuff cost thousands of dollars. How could Ava handle that? She turned the dress around and saw the big SAMPLE tag attached to it. Holy crap—it was from *Couture*'s closet. *Ava stole a dress?*

"Can't you find the water?" Ava asked. "I just put some in to chill." She came around the corner in time to see Callie stuffing the dress back into the closet.

"Oh" was all Ava said.

"It's from the fashion closet, right?" Callie confronted her.

Ava's face blanked out, her complexion suddenly as pale as the industrial-strength white paint on the dorm walls. She turned around and made a beeline back to the bedroom. Callie followed her, holding the dress. Ava sat down on the bed and cradled her head in her hands.

"Ava, it's okay. I'm not going to tell on you. You're my friend," Callie reassured her.

Ava looked up through her hands, her expression so pained that Callie would've done almost anything to take it back. Callie laid the dress on a chair and put her hand on Ava's shoulder. "Honey. I totally get it. That fashion closet, it just sits there with all those goodies in it. Like it's teasing us. All the models get to wear these pretty things, and the fashion editors make a ton of money and get freebies. Then there's Aynsley and her million-dollar wardrobe, and Nadine, who treats Aynsley's closet like a lending library. And then there's you and me, left out in the cold," Callie commiserated. "It's so hard not to feel like you're beneath everyone else."

Ava just sighed and looked at the dress. She was a tall girl, but it was like her guilt had shrunk her by a foot. Callie continued. "Trust me. I've thought of doing the same thing, but I can't because what I *really* need is something to wear to the Cutting Edge Gala. And I'm so *freaking* out. I mean, how am I supposed to look the part of a high-end designer?"

"By wearing something you made," Ava suggested quietly.

"That won't fly. I could tell by the way Lucy was

197

like 'We've got to make sure your look is beyond reproach.' She meant I should be wearing some established designer. Fine if you've got a Daddy Warbucks, but you and me, how are we supposed to compete? It's not like in that movie where they let Anne Hathaway borrow clothes every day. Can you imagine, 'Hey, Dieter, can you pick out a nice Gucci gown for me?' Yeah, right."

Ava laughed weakly. Callie giggled along with her. "It's not really that, though," Ava said. "Even when I wear designer stuff, they never look as good on me."

"You're so full of it," Callie teased her. "I'll bet this dress is a dream on you."

"I doubt it," Ava said.

"You haven't tried it on?"

"No way. What if I damage it?" Ava shuddered at the thought.

"Wasn't the whole point of taking it to wear it for something?" Callie paused, the wheels in her head turning: Ava on the phone when she came in. Something about this weekend. Her embarrassment. Now it made sense. She'd taken the dress to wear on a date. "I get it. You nabbed the dress to wear out with Reese. So you *are* going out this weekend? You should tell me these things. That's great," Callie squealed.

"Yeah, great," Ava said miserably.

Callie felt so bad for her friend. How could she be twenty-one, so pretty, and yet so nervous around guys? She'd seemed so happy when she'd met Reese, but maybe that was because Callie had been there, or because they'd been a little drunk. But to look at her now: She and Reese were going on a date—obviously somewhere seriously fancy to warrant such a dress—and Ava acted like she was going to a funeral.

"Well, Reese shouldn't be the only one to see you in this. Try it on," Callie demanded.

"I shouldn't," Ava said.

"You should. And if there's any problems with fit, I can pin it for you. That's what they do with the models. Reese will never know, nor will the people in the fashion closet—" Callie stopped short. "You are planning on bringing this back, right?"

"God, yes," Ava replied. "First thing Monday morning."

"You promise? I'd hate for something bad to happen to you."

"You and me both," Ava said glumly.

"Fine, you'll return it Monday morning. We'll both go in early, so I can be your lookout to make sure no one sees you."

"That's so sweet of you," Ava said. "But I can't let you get in trouble."

"Please, I'm good at being sneaky." For a second Callie thought of the Brooklyn silk-screen artist, but she quickly pushed him out of her head.

"There's no way I'm letting you risk anything," Ava said. "I got myself into this awful mess. I'll get myself out."

"It's not an awful mess. It's a dress. And one I want to see you in. Now," Callie insisted.

Ava started to hem and haw, but Callie put a finger to her lips and handed over the frock. Ava took it and shuffled to the bathroom. After five minutes, she still hadn't come out.

"You okay in there?" Callie called.

"Yeah. I'm just trying to be really careful."

"Does it fit?"

"I think so," Ava said in a small voice.

"Come on out."

Ava emerged from the bathroom and Callie sucked in her breath. The dress fit as if it had been made for her. The bodice was tight, showing off Ava's long, lean torso, and making the most of her small bust. The flare at the waist only emphasized how petite Ava was. And the color lit up all the pinks and roses in Ava's complexion.

"Oh. My. God," Callie said.

"What? That awful?" Ava moaned.

"You're like Cinderella, post–fairy godmother. You look beautiful."

"I do?" Ava asked with a shy smile.

"Yeah, and I have the perfect thing to go with this. Hang on." Callie raced upstairs to her dorm room, pulling out the thin purple leather belt she'd just bought. Yep, it was a perfect match for the dress. She also grabbed a pair of DKNY pink strappy sandals. When she returned, Ava was still standing in front of the mirror, staring at her reflection as though it belonged to someone she'd never seen before.

"Here, this'll make it a little less dressy, more funky," Callie said, tying the belt around Ava's waist. She held the shoes up to the netting. "Look, these match the petals perfectly. Try them on." Ava stepped into her shoes. "You should put a flower or two in your hair. For the full effect," Callie instructed her.

"Okay," Ava said a bit apprehensively.

"You look beautiful. Better than the models, even. I can't wait for Reese to see you. Can I be here when he picks you up?"

"Oh, yeah. Well, we'll probably meet in Long Island," Ava explained.

"You're going on a date in *Long Island*?" Callie looked confused.

"Well, no. I just have to go to my parents' house tomorrow and he's gonna be in the area, so he's picking me up there."

Callie felt a shot of disappointment—she wouldn't get to see her friend all dolled up, and if Nadine spent the whole weekend at Aynsley's, she'd be on her own until Sunday night. Never mind. She had plenty to do this weekend, finishing up the remaining silk-screen bags. "Well, you just take a picture for me," Callie said sweetly.

"I will," Ava agreed.

"You better. And you swear you'll give this back first thing Monday?"

"That," Ava said, looking relieved, "is a promise."

"To err is human, to forgive is divine."

Filed under: Fashionista > Style

The Fashionista is going to attempt to be even more divine than usual by pointing out, and forgiving, the hideous fashion sins she witnessed just this past weekend.

Friday night at <u>Le June</u>, the Fashionista spotted a starlet-who-shall-remain-nameless wearing a micromini with stockings and a garter belt, sans underwear. Can we please let this hideous trend die? It's been eons since we spied <u>Paris</u>'s or <u>Britney</u>'s privates, so if those fashionable flashers can commit to donning <u>La Perla</u>s, the rest of you have no excuse!

Then on Saturday afternoon at <u>Gagosian Gallery</u>»

in Chelsea, a certain Latvian supermodel (hint: she just landed a huge cosmetics deal and will soon have her face plastered all over the country) was spotted in denim cutoffs, four-inch Manolos, and a wife-beater with glittery suspenders. Now, the Fashionista appreciates a certain degree of creativity, but if one is a known "face of style," shouldn't one avoid dressing like a clown? Saturday night at Casa Mono was equally disappointing, when the Fashionista was horrified by a parade o' breasts. Never mind the to-the-chin cleavage (ladies, we know you're proud of your boobs, but show some restraint, please!). What was up with the plunging necklines and the peep-show side glimpses? If the Fashionista wanted to see naked breasts, she'd go to Saint-Tropez. Or buy a copy of *Playboy*. Sunday morning at church (the Fashionista's church—Barneys), I caught a glimpse of a fellow worshipper, a famous Manhattan socialite, *who should know better*, wearing a pair of terry-cloth shorts, with the words Squeeze Please over either butt cheek. The horror! And at Barneys! Is nothing sacred?

Sigh. The Fashionista forgives the aforementioned faux pas and trusts that the rest of my fellow fashionistas will wise up.

Your faithful Fashionista

17

The Most Notorious Rivalry in Fashion History

IT WAS THE dress that gave Aynsley the perfect opening. To be specific, it was a beaded silver strapless ankle-length bias-cut dress, designed by Alexandra Foxwood, of all people.

After an extended lunch hour on Wednesday afternoon, Callie strolled into *Couture* holding a lavender Bergdorf Goodman shopping bag aloft like it was some kind of trophy. Aynsley could tell she was trying to act casual, as if she shopped at Bergdorf's all the time.

Nadine looked up from her pile of menus. "What d'yah get?"

"Yeah, Cal. Since when do you shop at *Bergdorf*

Goodman?" Ava asked meaningfully.

"Oh, you know. The Cutting Edge Gala is next Friday—only a week and a half away. I thought I'd better get on it. Besides, they were having a sale. And this dress was calling my name."

"You just gonna stand there with your bags or you gonna show us what you bought?" Nadine asked impatiently. "Come on. I need a distraction from all this catering crap. Who knew figuring out the food for one party would be so much work?" she said.

"Yes, Callie, do share your fashion score," Aynsley encouraged.

Callie licked her lips and blinked several times. "Okay. But close your eyes. I want to put the whole outfit together for you."

Nadine and Ava quickly obliged. Aynsley sighed inwardly and played along.

"Okay, check it out."

Callie was holding the gown against her, allowing her tawny hair to drape over the shimmery fabric. Even thrown over her neck, the dress made her look at least half a foot taller, and the pewter Manolo slingbacks she'd put on her feet only added to the effect. Aynsley had to admit, at least to herself, the outfit was pretty dazzling.

"Wowza, now that is a dress!" Nadine exclaimed.

"And the shoes. Are those Manolos?" Ava asked.

Callie nodded triumphantly.

"Who's the designer?" Ava asked.

"It's Alexandra Foxwood, right?" Marceline answered as she entered the office looking springy in a peach Anna Molinari chiffon dress and kelly green sandals that looked like they were made out of grass. "Equal parts punk attitude and sexy style—just like Alexandra herself. You got this for the gala?"

Callie nodded.

"Ballsy choice. I can't wait till Isabel sees it. And so smart of you to go for a high neckline. Thanks to the Fashionista's rant about peekaboo cleavage, Isabel is on a new modesty kick." Marceline reached out to finger the beads of Callie's dress, then grabbed the price tag and raised an eyebrow. "Sixteen hundred. Good deal for couture. But I thought this was an *unpaid* internship."

Callie flushed. "But it's a once-in-a-lifetime—or maybe a *first*-in-a-lifetime—event so I thought I'd splurge." She was trying to look upbeat, but Aynsley could see a shadow of doubt darken her face.

"That's right," confirmed Aynsley, recognizing an opening. "This is just the kind of dress that every Bexley girl should have in her closet. You know, for all those formal parties at school."

"Right," Callie said shakily. "Good for all the parties."

Aynsley smiled. Formal parties at prep schools? Maybe prom, but other than that, the richer the student throwing the soirée, the more studiously casual the dress code. Aynsley had prep school friends from Los Angeles to Chicago to Boston, and among all of them, these days, it was $350 jeans—not evening gowns— that were all the rage.

"A good investment, then," Marceline said before leaving.

"So, what's the damage?" Nadine asked. "The dress plus the Manolos, I'm guessing two grand easy."

Callie suddenly looked queasy, as though Nadine hadn't asked her a simple question, but rather had shown her a picture of something disgusting: like a piece of roadkill, or a *Girls Gone Wild* video. Aynsley said nothing—she simply watched Callie squirm and waited patiently.

"How the hell are you going to pay for that?" Ava asked urgently.

Callie looked stricken, as though she might hurl, but then she took a few deep breaths and seemed to steady herself. "I charged it. It's not a big deal," she said through clenched teeth. She was staring hard at Ava, as if telepathically shouting for her to please shut up.

"I, for one, think it's a fantastic dress," Aynsley said. "Maybe it will get Isabel to rethink her ban on Foxwood."

"Huh?" Callie asked, her head spinning.

"Surely you know this story? It's fashion lore," Aynsley said smugly.

Callie turned pale. Aynsley detected a slight trembling in her hands. She paused, to savor the moment before elaborating. "It goes way back. Isa and Alexandra were friendly decades ago. That was when Alex was the doyenne of the London punk scene, hanging out with Malcolm McLaren, the Sex Pistols, and all. Isa was starting to make a name for herself as a young fashion editor in Paris. They met, became best friends, and then had some horrible falling out. Word is that Isa slept with Alex's boyfriend or vice versa. Isabel wrote something bitchy about Alexandra's collection, then Alex dissed Isabel in several interviews. They haven't spoken since. And when Isabel took over at *Couture*, she placed an unofficial *Couture* ban on Alexandra's designs. It's the most notorious rivalry in fashion history. That's why Marceline called the dress a ballsy choice."

"Oh" was all Callie could say.

"I'm sure it will be fine. Isabel probably won't even notice," Aynsley said, eating up every moment of this delicious exchange, and wanting more than anything to continue it. As she watched Callie's discomfort grow, she realized she now had the perfect opportunity to dig down beneath Callie's phony façade. "Speaking of the gala, and fashion history, I've done almost all of my interviews except yours, and Kiki wants them all done by this Friday, so the editors have next week to copy edit and fact check the copy. Why don't we do it now? We can hit the cafeteria for frozen yogurts and chat about your fashion pedigree."

"Okay," Callie said, looking bewildered. Aynsley almost felt bad for her. Bad luck buying a dress far beyond one's means that happened to be designed by Isabel's archenemy. And she probably bought the gown on clearance—which meant no returns. Then again, it was the girl's own fault. If she'd spent half the time studying up on *Couture* history that she did on sucking up, she might've known better.

"Let's hang your gorgeous gown in the closet so it doesn't get mussed. But keep the shoes on," Aynsley suggested. "It will be good to break them in before the party. And, besides, they look better with your outfit," she added, gesturing to the black silk tiered skirt and white wifebeater undershirt that Callie had embellished with bits of chain and straps of vinyl.

Downstairs, the cafeteria was quiet, just a few remaining late lunchers nibbling on salads. Aynsley bought them each a yogurt and found an empty booth near the windows in the back.

"Don't you just love Bergdorf's?" Aynsley asked. "The service is more refined than Barneys. Bendel's is also nice. I got this there," she said, twirling the sash on her kicky royal blue Stella McCartney minidress.

"It was nice," Callie said. "They were really helpful. I've never been to Barneys or Bendel's, though."

"Really?" Aynsley asked, jotting this down in her notebook, as if it were pertinent fashion information. "So where do you shop?"

"Um, you know. Here and there . . . sample sales," Callie explained.

"Sample sales, *really?*" Aynsley trilled. "Do they have good ones in Ohio?"

"Uh, some good ones. Marc Jacobs," Callie offered hopefully.

"Were you at the Marc by Marc Jacobs sale a few weeks ago?" Aynsley asked. She'd had to pull some strings to get access to that one and she knew Callie hadn't been invited.

"Oh, I meant back in Ohio," Callie replied.

"Is that right?" Aynsley said. She'd have to do some checking, but she was fairly certain that designers like Marc had sample sales in New York, London, Paris—maybe Los Angeles, but not Ohio. In a perverse way, Aynsley felt a little sorry for Callie. Her problem wasn't that she lived in the Midwest or that she couldn't afford designer clothing. In fact, Aynsley would've thought it was pretty damn cool that someone like Callie, faced with the fashion tundra that was Ohio, opted to make her own stuff. What made Callie pathetic was that she chose to lie, and did it so badly, when she didn't need to. *That* is what offended Aynsley.

"So, let's talk a little about Bexley Prep. Who are some of your famous alumni?"

"Uhh, I don't know," Callie sputtered. "I mean, I've got so much going on, I can't remember."

"Oh, really," Aynsley sighed knowingly. "At my school they constantly harped about famous grads—to motivate us, I suppose."

"Well, they did that, too, but I don't remember. Plus, the school's not that old, and aren't we supposed to be talking about fashion?"

"Just getting some background," Aynsley explained. "You said you learned to silk-screen there. From what

I understand, silk screening takes quite a bit of space and equipment. It's unusual that a prep school would have such an elaborate arts curriculum, no?" Aynsley didn't know if that was true. All she knew was that the point of schools like Dalton, Spence, and even funky St. Ann's was to make you arty enough on paper to impress Harvard and Brown—*not* to actually teach you how to make art.

Callie's eyes darted around the cafeteria. She shrugged. "We had a big art studio, so you could pretty much try anything you wanted. Drawing, painting, silk screening. There was a strong emphasis on the arts."

"I see. So you're going to be a senior. What are you thinking about college? What are your top schools?"

Callie held her hands up in the air. "No clue. I'll worry about that next year."

"What does your adviser say?" Aynsley pried.

"My what?"

"Surely you've been assigned a college adviser by now. In Manhattan, the whole college dance begins practically in toddlerhood, with wealthy parents hiring experts to get their babies into the right preschool. By ninth grade," she continued, "you get a personal college guidance counselor breathing down your neck to sign up for lacrosse or chorus, or to go build houses in

Mexico. Anything to pad your résumé, because just being a prep-school student, even a straight-A prep-school student, won't get you into Northwestern these days."

"If things go my way, I won't even go to college," Callie said, snapping out of her daze. "I'm not even out of high school and I'm going to have my designs in *Couture*."

"Which is a great start, but don't pin your hopes on that," Aynsley said. "One fashion spread does not a career make."

Callie glared at Aynsley as if she'd just blasphemed.

"Hey, I'm just telling it like it is," Aynsley insisted. "You might want to think about design school— FIT or Parsons."

Callie's expression softened. "I'd love to, but my parents, *you know*. They told me I had to get a 'proper' degree in like history or economics."

"I see," Aynsley said. "Try telling them that those schools are the Ivy League of design. Donna Karan graduated from Parsons." Aynsley was a little surprised to hear herself offering sincere and supportive advice to Callie, but for the first time, she had the sense that Callie was telling the truth. "So, let me confirm your background details. Since we'll be publishing your bio for the event, I want to be sure I've got all the facts. You learned to sew when you were three. And you've attended prep school since kindergarten, right?"

"Uh, just high school," Callie said.

"And you learned to silk-screen at school. Is that where you created your dead celebrity fabrics?"

"Right," Callie said. "Does all this matter?"

"Of course it does. But now, let's get to the important business: Who's styling you?"

"Huh?"

"On the night of the gala. Hair? Makeup?" Aynsley asked with a smirk.

"I hadn't really thought about that," Callie said, looking unsure of herself again.

"Well, you'd better think about it," Aynsley advised. "If you don't have the right hair and makeup, you'll look ridiculous in that dress. I'd go with an edgy look. Iron your hair stick straight, do your eyes dark and smoky, lips dramatic and red. I'll tell you what, let me call my guy in Soho. He does lots of celebs for premieres." Aynsley grabbed her BlackBerry and hit the number before Callie had the chance to say a word.

"Hi Trish. It's Sly Rothwell. I've got a favor to ask.

A friend of mine is going to be honored at the *Couture* Cutting Edge Designers Gala and she needs someone to style her. Can Marco squeeze her in next Friday night?" Aynsley paused. "You are a goddess. Yes, the name is Callie Ryan. Okay, six o'clock. Wonderful. No, Jules is back tomorrow. I'll tell him. Thanks, sweetie." Aynsley hung up the phone and smiled at Callie. "You're in."

"Wow, thanks," Callie said.

"You'll love Marco. He's not cheap, of course, but what's a couple hundred bucks more when you've already dropped two grand, right?" she asked with a haughty laugh.

Callie's face froze. Aynsley watched the conflicting emotions—fear, gratitude, embarrassment—play across her face. She simultaneously pitied and loathed the girl. All she had to do was be honest, say that she couldn't afford it, and Aynsley would've respected her. She might even have offered to pay for her, or charmed Marco into comping the appointment. But as long as Callie insisted on being a lying fake, Aynsley felt compelled to call her bluff.

Callie's gaze hardened as she put her mask back on. "That's great, Sly," she said with a forced smile. "Now, if you'll excuse me, I have to get back to work." Callie jumped up from the table, leaving her untouched yogurt melting in its bowl. Aynsley watched her scurry across the dining room. Satisfied with the interview, she smiled and snapped her notebook shut.

18
Amateur Mistakes

FRANKLY, NADINE DIDN'T give a flying you-know-what about whether the gazpacho should be served with mini manchego quesadillas or semolina cheddar twists or which seafood hors d'oeuvre she preferred. This was her third meeting with Clayton Company, and the caterer was droning on as though crab cakes versus sashimi was a life-threatening decision. Meanwhile, Nadine had been in this meeting since noon and was supposed to be back at *Couture* in less than an hour for yet another meeting with Lucy.

"I really have to get moving," Nadine said for the fifth time.

"Yes, yes. But first, tell me: crème fraîche or sour cream on the salmon canapés?"

He'd been asking her these kinds of questions all morning. As if Nadine had the slightest idea. "You know, we really trust you to make these decisions," she said, gathering up her papers. "That's why we chose your company over so many others."

The caterer looked sufficiently flattered, so Nadine made her escape. "Please fax over the final menu ASAP, so I can run it by my colleagues." Before he had a chance to object, Nadine was out the door.

Rather than run the risk of getting stuck in traffic, Nadine decided to take the subway back to work. She hustled down 14th Street as fast as her Baby Phat hot pants and platform sandals would carry her. Descending the subway stairs, she felt the onslaught of muggy, garbage-redolent air. Rats were dancing along the tracks. *The crap I go through,* she thought to herself, *and still they treat me like shit.* Five minutes later, the train arrived. Phew. She'd be back at *Couture* with time to grab the caterer's fax and maybe even wipe some of the underground grime off her face.

But as soon as the train pulled out of 34th Street, it suddenly stopped in the tunnel. When five minutes had passed, Nadine got a little antsy. The AC had gone off and the car was getting warm. Then ten minutes went by. Over the loudspeaker the conductor finally announced that the train ahead of them had stalled, and they'd be moving shortly. After twenty minutes, Nadine was ready to jump out the window and walk the tunnels. By the time she got to the *Couture* offices, forty-five minutes later, and ten minutes after the meeting had begun, she was covered in a sheen of sweat and in a full-on panic.

She raced into the conference room. "I'm so sorry I'm late. The caterer went long. The subway got stuck. It's been one of those days."

Lucy stared at her like she was speaking gibberish. "If you'll excuse us, Nadine, we're in the middle of a meeting."

"I'm sorry. I'll just take a seat." She glanced over at Aynsley, who shot back a sympathetic smile.

"I'm *afraid* you misunderstand," Lucy said, looking not afraid at all in a red power suit cut to reveal her surgically enhanced cleavage. "*We* are having a meeting. Not you."

"I just told you. It wasn't my fault I'm late. I was at the caterers' for two hours—you can call and ask—and then the subway got stuck."

Lucy stared at her, nostrils flaring. "Nadine, do you

know the difference between excuses and commitments? Commitments matter."

Nadine felt a prickle of anger surge up her spine. For chrissakes, she hadn't done anything wrong. Why was this bitch picking on her? She wanted to tell Lucy where to shove her lame-ass lectures. But she held it together. "I . . . I just finalized everything with the menu a full week in advance like you asked," she stammered. "Don't you need me to—"

"Ava has already briefed us on the caterer," Lucy interrupted. "Thankfully, someone has her act together."

Nadine turned to Ava, who bashfully held up the fax that Nadine had instructed the caterer to send. At least the blowhard had managed to do that in a timely fashion. Ava shrugged, her face painfully apologetic.

"So, as you can see," Lucy continued, "we won't be in need of your services. You're dismissed."

Nadine slunk out of the conference room, a tornado of emotions brewing inside her: shame, embarrassment, fury. It was all so unfair. This wasn't her fault at all. And the hair incident hadn't been entirely her fault either. But the whole staff hated her as though she'd been trying to sabotage the magazine or something. It wasn't true, but it didn't matter. She'd completely blown her internship. Maybe she should just quit and spend the rest of the summer back in Philly. She was over being a *Couture* patsy.

There was no point going back to the intern office. She didn't have anything to do. Instead, she grabbed her camera bag and made her way to the darkroom. She'd been surprised to discover that *Couture* even had a darkroom. Film and film processing were like dinosaurs in the age of digital, but apparently Isabel still preferred the look of film. So behind the photo department was a small studio, and in the back corner of the studio was a tiny darkroom that no one ever seemed to use.

As soon as she stepped inside and inhaled the chemical smell of the developing solutions, Nadine relaxed. She started printing the shots she'd taken over the last few weeks, getting completely lost in the magical process whereby negatives, plus light, plus paper, plus chemicals alchemized into images. There was a series of Ava that was truly amazing. Very stark black and white, almost Avedon-like, with Ava appearing both beautiful and mysterious in a way that she didn't seem in real life. Nadine knew that sometimes the lens caught subtleties the human eye missed. She printed a half dozen different shots of Ava, watching her face materialize in the developer. She couldn't wait to show these to the other girls.

While those prints dried on the line, she went to work on a shot of her and Julian in a liplock. It wasn't a picture she was too anxious to have floating around the office. Things were finally copacetic between her and Callie and she wasn't in any hurry to ignite more roommate wars. The prudent course was to burn the negative and be done with it. But Nadine Van Buren had always been allergic to the prudent course, so she arranged the negative in the enlarger. At the very least, the print was evidence of a wild night at Sly's that Nadine barely remembered—save for the bone-crunching hangover she'd woken up with the next day.

She swirled the print in the developer, seeing the kiss appear before her. "Yeah, honey," she told Julian as he materialized. "You think I'm hot. Admit it. Another notch in the old belt." She laughed out loud.

"Hello. Someone in there?" a subtly British male voice called out from the photo studio.

Nadine jumped. She had never been told specifically *not* to go into the darkroom, but suddenly she was scared she was going to get in trouble again. "Uh, yeah," she called out. "Let me get my stuff together and I'll leave."

"No need for that. It's cozy, but there's room for two. I've got some prints I need to make, so put your photo paper away for a tad and let me know if you've got anything in the bath."

Nadine put her photo paper away and opened the door. Standing in the doorway was a tall, thin guy with perfectly messy black hair and piercing blue eyes framed by gorgeous crinkling smile lines. He was wearing low-slung black jeans, beat-up navy suede Prada tennis shoes, and a tattered Ramones T-shirt. Nadine had to stop herself from gasping at his hotness. "Cheers," he said, entering the room and dropping his huge camera bag. "Sam Owens, staff photographer."

Nadine had heard about Sam—twenty-three years old, from England, in New York since he was eighteen, on *Couture*'s staff for a year now—but she'd never actually seen him. He always seemed to be out on a shoot somewhere glamorous. Sam cocked his head. "And you are—a professional darkroom squatter?"

Nadine laughed. Funny + Hot = Blistering. "I'm Nadine Van Buren. Resident whipping girl."

"Does it say that on your business card as well?"

"It would if they gave me a business card. I'm just a lowly intern, hiding out in the darkroom."

Sam chortled. "That bad, is it?"

"Oh yeah, I'm big-time *persona non grata* around here. Barely fit to take latte orders. I just got my ass chewed out by a publicist because I was late for a meeting, even though I was late because the caterer went on for too long and then the damn subway stalled."

"I see. Hard to say which is harder to bear, the subways in summer or *Couture* staffers in a snit. Never mind. Just do what I do: Picture them in their underwear."

Nadine giggled. Sam walked past her and looked at the photos she had drying on the line. "These yours?" he asked.

"Uh, yeah," Nadine replied, trying to summon some of her usual bravado.

He pulled one of the Ava shots down. "These are lovely," he said.

"You think so?" Nadine said, warming up as she moved in closer. He had a vine tattoo peeking out from his leather watchband, and he smelled like a mix of baby powder and sweat. Delicious.

"Definitely," Sam encouraged her. "You've got quite an eye. Why in God's name don't they have you working in the photo department?"

"We interns have to do whatever they tell us. And I was working in Photo at first," Nadine explained, "but then I guess I screwed up and got myself demoted."

"Another stalled subway?" Sam inquired, his eyes twinkling.

Nadine explained her hair situation, pulling off the Christian Dior black vinyl biker hat she'd borrowed from Aynsley to hide her lack of locks.

"I'd call that a happy accident. The short style really suits you," Sam said, eyeing her. "Not many women can carry off a pixie. Shame to hide it under a hat."

Nadine flung the hat into the corner and ran her fingers through her hair. "Better?" she asked, batting her eyes.

"Much," he replied. "And I'm sorry to hear you've had such a rough go of it. Sounds like you need someone in your corner."

"You're so right," Nadine said, leaning in and pushing out her chest. She wished it wasn't so dark in here, so Sam could see the full package. Then again, he was obviously interested in her, wanting to get in her corner and all that.

Sam turned back to the photos. He pulled down the one of her and Julian and studied it for a while. Nadine briefly regretted printing it, but then she reminded herself that guys always wanted you more if they thought they had competition—some kind of caveman thing.

He turned to her and with a small grin said: "I can see you didn't shoot this one."

"Oh, right. Because I'm in it?" Nadine said sarcastically.

"There's that, but mostly because the composition is shite and it's blurry, but not in a good, soft-focus way," he explained. "You wouldn't make such amateur mistakes, would you?"

"No, but I make other amateur mistakes," Nadine said with a naughty twinkle in her eye.

"Mind if I take a look at your contact sheets?" Sam asked her.

"Be my guest," Nadine offered.

He put the tiny rows of shots on the lightbox and peered at them through a magnifying loupe. Nadine took the opportunity to leer at his skinny ass, his jeans hanging off his narrow hips. She loved the whole emaciated punk arty look. Sam suddenly turned around to face Nadine. He was grinning again, as though he knew that she had been checking him out.

"Nadine. I've got an idea. We just scheduled an autumn coats shoot. Really sumptuous pieces, and we're doing it upstate in this very old-school lodge—dark wood, animal heads, and all that WASPy business. Would you fancy coming along?" Sam offered. "You could be my assistant. Maybe even shoot a roll or two on your own."

Nadine wanted to reach out and kiss the guy—and not just because she was grateful for his help. He was seriously do-able. And she could tell he was attracted to her: the invitation to a romantic lodge, the offer to be his assistant. She knew how to read between the lines, and she couldn't wait to spend some time with Sam in a different kind of dark room. Maybe they could, you know, photograph each other in some dirty positions. Her mind was so busy racing ahead that she hardly heard Sam say that he'd square it all with Kiki because it was a damn shame to waste a budding talent like Nadine's.

"Bloody hell, look at the time," he said. "I've got to get these prints done for Dieter now. If you'll excuse me, I'll be in touch about the shoot. We'll get you out of the dungeon in no time."

"Thanks, Sam," Nadine said, licking her lips suggestively. "I'm really looking forward to us working together."

She grabbed her prints from the line. Then she bent over to put them in her portfolio, lingering a while so Sam could admire the view—even though he seemed too busy to notice. It was only when Nadine let herself outside the studio that she actually *heard* what Sam had said about her—she had talent. Of course, she'd known that all along, but it felt pretty damn good to have someone at *Couture* finally say so.

19

Ava on the Edge

AVA SAT IN the intern office late Thursday afternoon, nervously tapping her strappy DKNY pink sandals against the floor. Actually, they were Callie's sandals—Ava had them on long loan. Ava marveled at her luck: finding a friend as generous as Callie who also happened to wear the same size shoes and clothes. But her happy reverie was quickly jolted by a familiar burst of guilt. If Callie had known the truth about Ava's supposed big date last weekend, Ava doubted she'd have been so generous with her footwear or so discreet about the Alexander McQueen dress.

At least she'd managed to return the gown Monday

morning with no one the wiser. Ava smoothed down an invisible crease in her white J. Crew trousers and straightened the straps of her pale pink Callie Ryan camisole. She felt like she was going to jump out of her own skin. How much longer could she keep all this up?

"Hello, Miss Ava Barton." Nadine was standing in the doorway to the office, a mile-wide grin spread across her face. She'd disappeared from the offices after Lucy's nasty dismissal—to lick her wounds, Ava guessed. Lucy had been awfully hard on her, but from Nadine's current cheery demeanor, Ava wondered if she'd been licking a few mid-afternoon martinis.

"Hey, Nadine," Ava said cautiously. "I'm so sorry about before. When the menu fax came in, I just grabbed it without thinking. I told Lucy you were probably just running late at the caterer's, but she flew into a rage. I tried to explain that you'd been the one to get the menu in order," she added, "but she was being completely unreasonable." Ava picked the caterer's fax off her desk. It was full of red marks. "And if it makes you feel any better," she offered, "Lucy made dozens of changes to the menu and made *me* talk to the caterer. He practically bit my head off on the phone."

"That," Nadine said, taking a seat next to Ava and kicking her feet up onto the desk, "is probably my fault.

I told the guy to decide. I mean if I knew the difference between sour cream and crème fraîche, I'd be the frigging caterer."

Ava shook her head and laughed. "I think Lucy would've vetoed half the stuff no matter what was on it. Making us miserable makes her feel powerful," she said with a sigh. "But I'm glad you're not mad at me. I was worried about you. Especially when I couldn't find you after the meeting."

"Oh, don't worry about little old me," Nadine said with the old swagger back in her voice. "I was working in the darkroom with Sam Owens, the staff photographer."

Ava's smile was genuine. "That's great, Nadine."

"Sam said I've got talent. He's gonna set Kiki and her uptight minions straight."

"He's really respected in the industry," Ava said knowingly. "I mean, around here."

"And he's a whole new level of hot," Nadine added. "Speaking of hot guys, there's something I want to ask you. Are Sly and Callie around?"

"They're in the conference room drawing up seating charts," Ava explained.

"Cool, because this is kind of personal."

Nadine got up and closed the door, and Ava felt a ripple of fear.

"So, I gotta know," Nadine said with a mischievous grin. "Who's that hot guy you were with last week?"

"Huh?"

"The guy, or rather, *the man*, you're seeing."

"You mean Reese? We just met. We haven't really gone out," Ava said. "Much to Callie's disappointment." When Ava had told her this morning that their "date" had fallen through, Callie had acted as though she herself had been stood up or something.

"Oh, come on now. I saw you and the Silver Fox canoodling last Friday afternoon. You were looking pretty hot and heavy. But man, that guy looks old enough to be your father. You got a daddy complex?"

Ava's face went scarlet. "I don't know what you're talking about," she stammered.

"I saw you, after you left early to go to your so-called doctor's appointment. You were at Palais, drinking wine with the guy. Don't even try to bullshit me and say it wasn't you," Nadine pressed her. "You were wearing Callie's skirt. Only one of *those* in the world."

Ava took a few deep breaths and forced herself to look Nadine in the eye. "Oh, *that's* what you're talking about," she said, trying to sound casual. "That wasn't my boyfriend."

"Sure looked like it."

"You totally misinterpreted it," Ava said, her mind leaping one pace ahead of her mouth. "That guy was a new designer I was meeting with—to talk about his collection for the magazine."

"He didn't look like a new designer," Nadine said quizzically. "He looked like an old one, like Calvin Klein."

"Well, he is, I guess, older. But he's just opened a showroom and I was going to check it out, talk to him. I wanted to pitch a piece about him to Kiki, but I had to, you know, meet with him, see if his stuff was *Couture*-worthy." Ava knew she was babbling and closed her mouth. *Shut up,* she told herself.

Nadine puckered her lips in deep thought. "Well, that makes a little more sense. I was having a hard time picturing you out with some sugar daddy. I gotta admit, as unlikely as your whole never-been-kissed thing is, it feels more likely than you having an affair with some married guy."

Oh, God, Ava thought to herself, *do I have MISTRESS written all over me?* "No affair. No married guy. I swear on my mother's health," Ava insisted.

"Still, it didn't look like a business lunch. Or a preliminary meeting," Nadine pressed on. "The way you two had your heads all close together, I think the guy has a major thing for you."

"It was windy," Ava cried desperately. "He had to lean in to hear me. And he ordered the wine. I just had half a glass to be polite."

"Okay, chill," Nadine said, looking taken aback at the force of Ava's words. "I believe you, about the affair."

Ava suddenly felt a second wave of panic. "You didn't tell anyone about it, did you?" she asked quietly. "Aynsley? Callie? Kiki?"

"Nah, I wanted to check it out with you first. But why so top-secret if the geezer's just some wannabe designer?"

Relief washed over Ava. "I didn't want to bring it up, just in case nothing comes of it. I'm still not sure if it's going to work out."

Nadine stared at her intently. Ava had the sense that she was a hunk of ice and Nadine was a blowtorch. Any second now and Ava was going to dissolve into a puddle.

"I dunno, Ava. Something smells a little fishy."

"Maybe the last few weeks have made you paranoid," Ava suggested.

"Hello, ladies," Kiki said, knocking on the door and poking her head in the office. Ava was grateful for the interruption. "Have you finalized the menu?" Kiki asked.

"It's done," Ava replied.

"And Aynsley and Callie are doing seating?"

"Yes, they're in the conference room," Ava explained.

"Great. If you're done, Ava, you should really get downtown. The showroom closes at six and you'll want time to see him in his element before you do the interview."

"I'm on my way out now," Ava replied, practically holding her breath. All she had to do was square things with Nadine before she left.

"Chop, chop, then," Kiki said and disappeared.

"See," Ava said, turning back to Nadine. "I'm going to the showroom now. To do an interview. With the designer."

Nadine gave her a curious glance, then shrugged. "Cool. So you pitched this guy, and they bit?"

"Something like that," Ava replied. "I'm supposed to go hang out in his showroom, take notes, and write them up for the fashion department."

Nadine's hard gaze relaxed into a smile. "You're really moving up around here," she said.

It was true. Never in a million years had Ava dreamed that her internship at *Couture* would be anything like this. She'd expected to be treated like an underling, like a nothing, and instead, she was getting assignments befitting a staffer. She thought of Nadine and her troubles with Kiki and Lucy and she suddenly felt guilty about her own success.

"Again, I'm so sorry about the meeting today—and about all the treatment you've been suffering through," Ava said. "If there's anything I can do to help out, let me know."

"Don't you worry about me. I'm gonna be just fine around here," Nadine said with a grin.

Ava remembered Nadine's humiliated expression after Lucy booted her from the conference room earlier that afternoon. "Are you sure?" she asked her.

Nadine licked her lips and then exploded into mirthful laughter. "Okay, Ava. You told me your secret, so I'll tell you mine. Sam Owens took a shine to me. He asked me to come on a photo shoot next week as his assistant. He's gonna take me under his wing. Actually, I'd like him to take me under more than his wing, if you know what I mean?"

"That's awesome, Nadine. I'm so glad. You're a great photographer."

"That's right. I am," Nadine agreed. "About time somebody around here noticed. Which reminds me, I wanted to show you these photos. I feel like I captured something in you, something hidden and secretive."

"You did?" Ava felt like a guilty mistress all over again. Cameras couldn't really reveal secrets—could they?

"Check this out," Nadine said, offering up the photos. "I don't know what it is. This picture feels like it captures you on the verge of something. You're you, but also someone else. I can't explain it."

Ava looked at the print and exhaled in relief. It was just a picture of her, although it did look different from the Ava who stared back at her from the mirror every day. Nadine snatched the picture back.

"I want to frame it for you. A gift. I'm gonna title it *Ava on the edge*."

Tears welled up in Ava's eyes and she reached out to hug Nadine.

"Okay, okay," Nadine said, a little surprised by the show of emotion. "Don't go getting my top all wet."

"Sorry," Ava said with a laugh. She just felt so lucky all of a sudden. But deep down Ava couldn't help but wonder if her luck was about to run out.

20
Let It All Hang Out

CALLIE HAD JUST left the Conrad Publishing building when her cell phone chimed. She glanced at her caller ID—it was Julian.

"Did you miss me?" Callie cooed into the phone.

"Terribly," Julian answered. "I was thinking of you and our little picnic the entire flight home yesterday, which made for a—how shall I put this delicately?—uncomfortable eight hours."

Callie giggled, picturing Julian in first class and in need of a cold shower.

"Sure, laugh at a man when he's down," Julian said. "When can I see you? Are you free now?"

For a minute, Callie thought of that *Rules* book. Last-minute dates weren't encouraged. Then again, it was a Tuesday night and Julian had only just got back from Europe. "As a matter of fact, I am," Callie said, crossing 42nd Street. "I just finished an epic project for the *Couture* Cutting Edge Gala with your sister. The big day is almost here!"

"Then you must need a drink, badly. Why don't we meet at the Spotted Dog. West Village."

"When?"

"Now."

Callie glanced down at her outfit: her multifabric micromini—the one she'd worn on her first day at *Couture*—paired with a navy bandeau top and one of her new menswear jackets. Without the jacket, the outfit was definitely cute enough for a date.

"Okay. Where's the Spotted Dog?" she asked him.

Julian rattled off an address and said he'd be there in fifteen minutes, which Callie knew meant half an hour. It was a beautiful night, not too humid, the setting sun painting the sky lavender, orange, and peach. She decided to walk downtown, maybe even stop at Loehmann's in Chelsea for a quick browse.

When Callie arrived at her destination an hour later, she was slightly annoyed to find that Julian had chosen some pub. He always seemed to know the hot places to eat—the hole-in-the-wall taquería that Natalie Portman frequented, the best wine bar in the Village. But for once, couldn't he take her to Gramercy Tavern or Daniel or one of the other places the Zagat guide raved about? Her friends from Ohio were constantly asking if she'd eaten at the restaurants they read about in *Us* weekly, and her unsubstantiated Catherine Zeta-Jones sighting at Peter Luger's hadn't completely impressed them.

Julian was sitting at the bar, looking all sun-kissed and sexy, even more handsome than she'd remembered from the week before. He was wearing a pair of faded Levi's, a Comme des Garçons gray T-shirt, and a new suede jacket. When he spotted Callie, he put down his half-drunk pint of beer, slid down from his barstool, and brushed a kiss across her lips. She thought of their afternoon in the park, and what might've happened had Kiki not chosen that moment to call.

"Thinking dirty thoughts?" Julian asked.

"Don't flatter yourself," Callie replied breezily, even though that's exactly what she'd been doing.

Julian led her to a wooden table, explaining that the Spotted Dog was the hottest gastropub in the city, having been written up in all the papers for its gourmet bar food and great selection of beers. It was run by the guys behind Babel, Luna, and Novo.

"I'll take your word on that," Callie said. She hadn't heard of those places, though she wasn't about to say so. And beer was gross. Plus it made you fat. She ordered a Kir Royale, remembering that Isabel had ordered one herself when she took the interns to lunch a few weeks back. Julian told the waiter to bring out some duck eggs, oysters, and calves' livers—*whatever happened to potato skins and mozzarella sticks?* she wondered—while Callie filled him in on all the drama of the last week: Her bag being crashed into the Cutting Edge feature; her photo shoot for the issue shot by *Couture*'s staff photographer, Sam Owens; her interview with Aynsley.

"I should go out of town more often," Julian said with a flirtatious grin. "Sounds like good things happen when I'm not here to distract you."

"Better things happen when you're here to distract me. In fact, it was because of Williamsburg." Callie stopped herself. She'd almost blurted that it was because of Williamsburg that she'd found the silk screens. Actually, part of her wanted to tell Julian about her predicament. Maybe he could tell her what to do.

"Because of Williamsburg what?" Julian asked.

"Did you meet some other guy on your little shopping jaunt?"

Callie laughed. Sort of, but not in the way he thought. "No, I was just going to say that I drew a lot of inspiration from that trip. I really loved it out there. It's weird, but I feel like my whole style has evolved since that day."

"Uh-huh," Julian said. He waved the waiter over and ordered another round of drinks.

"So, tell me about Europe. Did you get into any trouble?" Callie asked before hesitantly nibbling on a duck egg.

"Who me? No. I just relaxed on the beach, caught up with friends, ate my weight in foie gras."

Callie looked surprised. "You mean you didn't do anything wild—like steal a yacht with Nanette Lise?"

Julian rolled his eyes. "You shouldn't believe everything my sister says."

"So, it's not true, then?"

He tilted his head to the side and smiled his wolfish grin. "It's true, but you shouldn't believe old Sly. She's sneaky, that one. How's she doing at work? I'm surprised she hasn't been packed off to Umbria yet. I've heard that Gregory and Cecilia aren't all that pleased with her."

Callie felt a strange tug of loyalty toward Aynsley. She had, after all, been nice enough to get Callie an appointment with her stylist, though Callie planned to cancel it. Two thousand for a dress and shoes was one thing. Four hundred bucks to get her hair ironed straight and her makeup done was another. She'd decided to get a blowout from the Jean Louis David place and, at Ava's suggestion, have her makeup done at the Bobbi Brown counter at Saks before the event.

"She's doing okay. She knows a lot about fashion. And parties," Callie explained. "And she's helping with the guest list for the Cutting Edge Gala."

"Excellent, then I have an in," Julian crowed. "I'll see you in your moment of glory."

"If you're lucky," she teased.

"Oh, you do know how to torment a guy," Julian said with a wink.

"I try. So, you didn't see any girls in Europe?" Callie asked pointedly.

"I saw lots of girls. I was in France, land of topless bathing—everyone from the nubile teenagers to the wrinkled grandmothers let it all hang out. And let me tell you, there are some breasts you want to see and others you'd really rather not." Julian shriveled his nose and grimaced in mock horror. Then he leaned in and ran a finger up Callie's arm to the tip of her bandeau top. "You're the only one I want to see topless," he leered.

Callie grabbed her drink and gulped it, hiding her smile in the glass. At first, she hadn't been so sure that Julian really liked her. She'd heard stories from Aynsley about what a player he was and how he typically dated heiresses and models. She'd intimated in that subtle Aynsley way of hers that Callie was no one special to him. And the sparks had been less than hot on their first date. But after their makeout session in the park, and tonight, Callie thought he could really be into her. Maybe even fall in love with her. She imagined bringing Julian back to Ohio, showing him off to her friends from school. Well, maybe not her friends from school. He still thought she was a prep-school kid, but she suspected that Julian wouldn't really care if she told him the truth. After all, he liked the grungy parts of Brooklyn and the funky gastropubs. He wasn't a snob like his sister.

Julian's cell phone rang. He looked at the caller ID. "Do you know what area code 610 is?" Callie shook her head and Julian picked up the phone.

"Hello." He paused. "Who is this?" He turned to Callie and mouthed "Nadine" as he shrugged his shoulders.

Why was Nadine calling Julian? Callie wondered. She hadn't told anyone they were going out tonight. She hadn't known herself until a few hours ago.

"Sorry, Nadine, I can hardly hear you. I'm sorry. What? What'd you say about a picture? Who wants you?" Julian looked perpexed. "Did you need to talk to Callie—she's right here."

Julian handed the phone to Callie. "Hey, Nadine," Callie said. There was no reply. "Hello." The line went dead. "I think she hung up."

Julian shook his head. "She's probably drunk. Every time I see her, she's completely wasted."

"The girl does like to party. And she's found the perfect partner in your sister," Callie said cattily.

"Yes, but the key difference is that Sly knows how to hold her liquor. She really should stop boozing with Nadine. I mean, Sly's supposed to be getting her act together this summer. The last thing she needs is to be pulled down by some immature child."

Part of Callie wanted to defend Nadine, but the other part was glad that Julian thought she was a loser. Nadine was always bragging about how no guy could resist her, but here was Julian Rothwell, one of the most eligible bachelors in the city, and he wasn't interested in Nadine or in any of Aynsley's socialite friends. He wanted Callie.

"Now," Julian said, licking his lips. "Let's dispense with the chat about my sister and her loser cohorts and get back to more important matters, like . . . when am I going to see you topless?"

21

The Mystery of the Couture Mole

IT WAS TEN a.m. Wednesday morning and Nadine was already on her tenth pair of boots. She sighed dramatically, listening to the sound of her exhalation echo off the walls of *Couture*'s shoe closet, which was a "closet" in the way that Aynsley's mansion was an "apartment."

In a few months, duplicates of the same luxury footwear currently strewn across the floor would be gracing the feet of the richest, most fashionable women in the world. For now, they were all Nadine's. Between the Chanel crocodile knee-highs, Prada brushed leather riding boots, Gucci slouch spiked heels, Dior do-me stilettos, and Coach stacked-heel Oxfords,

Nadine figured that she'd tried on at least $10,000 worth of goods. Which was fun. For half an hour. Now she was bored shitless again. Lucy had kicked her off the Cutting Edge Gala committee, so while Callie, Ava, and Sly were down at the Apple Store prepping for the big event in two days, Nadine was sitting on her ass. Or trying on shoes.

She kept thinking about Sam and their upcoming rendezvous. It was the bright spot in her life right now—well, that and her nights out with Sly, always good for a laugh and a hookup. Who'd it been last night? She couldn't even remember the guy's name. Will or Bill or Phil? The boys blended together into a blob of preppy uptown wealth, and they were all obviously fascinated by an exotic urban specimen such as herself.

Sam wasn't like that. He was sophisticated. He was hot. He was funny. And he was her ticket out of *Couture* purgatory. Only problem was, he was nowhere to be seen. Ever since she'd met him for the first time last week, she'd been going to the darkroom each day, hanging sexy shots of herself on the line and hoping he'd barge in, in that adorable way of his. No such luck. She'd ambled by the photo department every chance she'd had, but still no sign. He'd said he'd be in touch about the shoot, but when exactly was that going to be?

Nadine sighed and replaced the boots. Didn't want to get in trouble for mussing the pretty shoes. Too bad Nadine wore a dainty size seven. If the samples weren't all nines, she'd have had to help herself to a pair of those really hoochie Steve Madden boots.

As soon as she closed the shoe closet, she bumped into a red-faced Kiki, her blond highlighted hair standing on edge like she'd been electrocuted. "Where the hell have you been?" Kiki asked, uncharacteristically nonplussed.

"In the bathroom," Nadine replied indignantly. Okay, she'd been slacking in the shoe closet, but that was no reason for Kiki to throw so much 'tude.

"We're having an emergency staff-wide meeting," Kiki informed her.

"You want me to come?" Nadine asked, licking her lips at the prospect of some action.

"I said *staff*, not interns," Kiki replied. "I need you to answer the phones. The receptionist called in sick, and the editorial assistant we'd put up front has to come to the conference room. Isabel wants the *entire* staff present."

"Sounds serious. What's going on?" Nadine asked.

Kiki eyed her bitchily. "Never you mind. Get to the phones *tout de suite*. Do you know how to work them?

If not, there's an instruction manual in the drawer. Go now! And bring your stuff. You'll be there the rest of the day."

"Okay."

"And do you have a jacket or something?" Kiki asked her.

Nadine looked down at her Necessary Objects black lace babydoll dress, an outfit that was as business-appropriate as Nadine Van Buren got. It wasn't her fault that her 34-Cs so amply filled out the tiny bustline. She stared at Kiki. "No. Why? Do you think I'll be cold?" she asked, daring Kiki to diss her.

Kiki didn't blink. "You look a little cheap, is all, but if that's the image you want to project, I don't have time to argue with you." And with that, she was off.

Nadine made her way to the intern office, grabbing her bag and Sly's white cashmere throw, which her perennially cold friend left draped over her office chair. She was cursing that frigging Kiki. As she wove through the *Couture* hallways toward the reception area, she could smell the buzz in the air. Everyone was talking. Something about "style"—whatever that meant. At *Couture*, wasn't everything about style?

"What's going on?" Nadine asked Marceline as she hustled by.

"None of your business," Marceline huffed and disappeared into the conference room.

For the fiftieth time this week, Nadine fought the urge to up and quit. She took a deep breath and reminded herself that everything would change soon. She'd go on the shoot with Sam, maybe have a fun roll in the country hay, and come back to the office with proof that she was the next Demarchelier. But first she had to figure out the damn phones. For an hour, Nadine fumbled through the system, accidentally hanging up on at least half a dozen people, while sending many more to the wrong extensions. She'd been yelled at by irate callers more times than she cared to count. Like it was her fault. The system had more buttons than a NASA computer. Finally, when she was starting to get the hang of it, the meeting ended. She knew this because she got bitched out by Dieter for putting a call through without asking who it was and without waiting on the line to make sure she'd connected it to the right extension. Next time a call came for him, she waited on the line, but didn't disconnect right away, frantically trying to find the right button to push. She accidentally hit Mute, thereby discovering how easy it was to stay on the line and listen in on a conversation. Which was how she found out exactly what was going on.

"That bloody rag *Style* scooped us again," Kiki was hissing into the phone, clueless that Nadine was listening. "First they got to Eamon Sinds. And now it turns out that they've got a big feature on jeweled military wear, which is what we crashed in when Isabel negged houndstooth. We've got a fashion spy."

Nadine's skin prickled with excitement. *A spy?* Some intrigue is exactly what she needed. Next, she eavesdropped on a conversation Dieter was having with a stylist. "If you ever vant to vork at *Couture* again, you vill tell me vat you know," he threatened.

The stylist was all insulted. "Why would I do such a thing?" she cried. "It would be career suicide to forsake *Couture* for *Style*. And Isabel is a friend!"

"Isabel believes it's somevone on the inside," Dieter hissed. "So everyvone is a suspect. Even me."

A little while later, Nadine listened to a conversation between Marceline and Kiki.

"Do you think it's an outsider?" Marceline asked.

"Dieter does. But Isabel doesn't," Kiki explained. "So far there are two known instances, the Sinds thing and the military spread, and we had entirely different models, stylists, and hair and makeup people working on those," she added. "So it doesn't make sense that it came from someone who's not on staff."

"Could it be someone from advertising?" Marceline asked. "That woman Cynthia used to work at *Style*."

"I suppose, but what incentive does she have?" Kiki mused. "If we lose ad pages, she gets screwed. I think it's someone on editorial. Someone Isabel has shit on one too many times."

Nadine quietly disconnected. She had to agree with Kiki. Knowing how the hierarchy worked around here, she could easily imagine someone on the low end of the totem pole getting even by leaking *Couture*'s lineup to *Style*. Not that Nadine would ever do anything like that. That was just bratty. Besides, if she wanted revenge, she'd make damn sure that Kiki and company knew who was gunning for them.

But it wasn't revenge Nadine was after. It was vindication. Everyone around her seemed to think that she was incapable of doing anything right. Now she had two ways to prove them wrong. Soon enough, with Sam's help, she would show everyone what a fabulous photographer she was. And in the meantime, she was going to solve the mystery of the *Couture* mole. After all, as editor in chief of her school's newspaper, she'd been both top shutterbabe and hotshot reporter. She knew how to investigate a story. *Ahem,* hadn't she single-handedly brought down her school cafeteria's food contractor by proving that there was no beef in the hamburgers? She could solve this little mystery in a snap.

In fact, she already had some leads. Being so resentful herself all these weeks, she'd developed a nose for sniffing out other staffers' grudges. Like Nelson. He was the copy chief who wanted to move over to editing articles, but no one would let him. She'd heard Kiki snipe that the guy had no sense of fashion or nuance so there wasn't a snowball's chance in hell that he'd get promoted. In fact, Kiki had told Aynsley the guy had a better shot of getting a job somewhere low-rent like *Style*! She didn't know if Nelson knew all of that, but if he did, that was certainly an incentive to become a *Style* spy. Then there was Wanda, one of the fashion closet girls. She always seemed to be bitching about Isabel and threatening to quit for a lesser magazine where she'd be treated like a queen.

Nadine opened the desk drawer and rifled through it for a pad of paper and a staff directory. She wrote down the name of each staff suspect, putting little stars next to the ones who smelled especially guilty or had likely turncoat motivations. She spent the rest of the afternoon listening in on as many conversations as she could. Even though Kiki had warned the staff to keep quiet—the last thing they needed was for this to wind up on Page Six—everyone was gossiping about the spy. At the end of the day, Nadine had a stack full of notes, a handful of suspects, and a sense that she might end this summer accomplishing something after all.

"In the future, everyone will be famous for fifteen minutes."

—Andy Warhol

Filed under: Fashionista > Style

What would you do for your fifteen minutes? The Fashionista has been pondering that question a lot of late, watching as various would-be designers, models, starlets, and <u>American Idols</u> bare their fangs and sharpen their claws for a piece of the spotlight.

How far would you go in pursuit of fame? Would you spread your cash around to win friends (as a certain <u>Harvard</u>-bound <u>Dalton</u> grad did last year in an attempt to curry favor with the "right people")? Would you spread nasty lies to destroy your competition (as a certain Argentine model did, looking to disgrace a fellow » mannequin)? Or would you shove a friend aside to make sure that you were first (as a certain <u>Couture</u> beauty editor did when she literally shoved a colleague who scored a guest spot on the <u>Today</u> show)?

Honestly, the Fashionista just can't understand what all the fuss is about. I've experienced fame, and here's a secret: It's overrated. It inspires predatory <u>paparazzi</u> and equally hungry hangers-on—*who are all*, in a word, *tiresome*. Success, on the other hand, is a worthy alternative to all kinds of celebrity. It's the stuff that drives that passionate <u>start-up jewelry designer</u> on the <u>Lower East Side</u> and that obscure <u>milliner up in Harlem</u> who re-creates vintage-era hats simply because he cannot bear to see a fashion gem tossed in the garbage. Are either of them famous? Hardly. On the road to celebrity? Doubtful. But they're already wildly successful in a way that most of us never will be.

Darlings, trust me, don't be seduced by the lure of notoriety. After all, there's a reason the Fashionista remains anonymous.

Your faithful Fashionista

22
Queen of the Velvet Rope

AYNSLEY REACHED HER arms over her head and stretched into a deep forward bend. It had been three weeks since her last private yoga session with Vikram, and her hamstrings were protesting from neglect. She examined her hands against the glistening white backdrop of the Apple Store. Her nails were a mess. *She* was a mess. How the hell did working stiffs manage to do the nine-to-five thing, have a social life, stay well groomed, and sleep? After spending the last two days chained to Lucy Gelson's side, Aynsley had a newfound respect for the rat race, and a newfound sense that she was never meant to run it. Not that she hadn't enjoyed working the phones the last few days, telling all her friends about Friday night's soirée, which she was certain was going to be *the* talked-about event of the summer. She had a knack for party promoting, that was for sure, but the fun part—talking on the phone and gossiping about who was attending the event (Nicky: yes. Paris: no. J.Lo: yes. Gwen: no.)—was only half of it. Drawing up Excel spreadsheets, coordinating with the security company, sitting on hold while waiting to talk to the assistant to the assistant of Gwyneth's publicist: That part was pure drudgery. It was a good thing the gala was coming up, because Aynsley was in serious need of a party.

After a quick sun salutation, Aynsley picked the lint off her Katayone Adeli skinny black trousers, adjusted the straps of her Christian Lacroix racer-back blouse, slipped on her Kenzo ballet flats, and went downstairs where the black Town Car that Lucy had ordered was waiting to take her home. (Ever the calculating social climber, Lucy had given Callie and Ava cab fare back to their dorm. Why waste private service on nobodies?) Aynsley grabbed her BlackBerry out of her white leather Tods Roxy and called Nadine's cell. No answer. She tried *Couture*, and when no one picked up the interns' extension, she hit zero for the operator. She'd make the receptionist track her down.

"*Couture.*"

Aynsley paused a beat. That didn't sound like the squeaky snoot of a receptionist. It sounded like—

"Oh, heavy breathing. Very sexy," the voice said sarcastically.

"Van Buren?"

"Sly, is that you?"

"Indeed. What are you doing answering the phones? Wait, never mind. It's six. Can you get out of there?"

"Sure, I was staying to do some investigating. There's a mole."

"Hadn't you best discuss that with your dermatologist?"

"Not that kind of mole. A spy. It's a long story, but you're not gonna—"

"Save it," Aynsley said, cutting Nadine off. "I'm driving uptown right now and will be outside the office in ten minutes. We'll have some drinks at my place and go somewhere mellow. This work thing is exhausting."

As the car pulled up in front of the Rothwell residence, Nadine finished filling Aynsley in on the spy business. Aynsley feigned interest—she could see that her friend was all juiced to play high-fashion Nancy Drew and solve the *Couture* crime. Anything to distract Nadine from her pity party was a good thing because, frankly, Aynsley was getting tired of hearing her friend's I'm-such-a-victim tirade. Initially, she'd tried to be supportive. She personally knew the hell of being a *Couture* fall girl. But it was going on four weeks now and Nadine was getting to be a bit of a bore. Pour a pair of cocktails down the girl's gullet and it was like putting the sob-story podcast on repeat. Aynsley was desperate to delete it.

Aynsley and Nadine trudged up the brownstone stairs and rang the bell. Aynsley left her keys at home most days—someone was always there to let her in—but she'd called ahead to Marta, just to make sure, and to request a light dinner. All she'd eaten today were two pieces of sashimi. Lucy, the last living person still doing Atkins, wouldn't let them order sushi with rice. Marta swung open the door, dressed not in her black-and-gray uniform but in one of the flowery dresses she favored. To Aynsley, she looked like one of Cecilia's busy sofas come to life.

"Taking the night off?" Aynsley trilled. "Big date?" This was their usual joke. Marta was about sixty.

Marta swatted Aynsley on the head with a copy of

her Spanish soap opera magazine and gave Nadine the fish eye. Aynsley knew from her own experience what Marta thought of the way girls dressed today—she criticized Aynsley's outfits in a way no one else would dare—and lately, she'd been complaining to Aynsley about how whorishly Nadine dressed.

"I supposed to get off early on Wednesdays, but I have to wait for you to come home," Marta complained.

"Sorry," Aynsley said, breezing past. "I thought Jules would be back. Did you fix us supper? I'm famished. "

"On the kitchen counter," Marta said, walking down the steps and toward the subway station.

Aynsley and Nadine sauntered into the kitchen, where Marta had laid out a selection of prosciutto, Parmesan cheese, smoked salmon, olives, and Eli's French bread, along with a big bowl of fresh cherries. Yum. She had to remember to score Marta some nice moisturizer from the beauty closet.

"So you see," Nadine was babbling on, "I've got it nailed down to Nelson, Wanda, Amelia, and my wild card, Dieter."

"Dieter. Why would Dieter blab to *Style*?" Aynsley asked, grabbing a bottle of Pinot Grigio from the wine fridge. "Isabel is his meal ticket."

"Exactly. Maybe he wants to get rid of her, so he can take over the magazine."

Aynsley popped an olive into her mouth and chewed. "Dieter would never be allowed to take over *Couture*."

"But he's number two on the masthead," Nadine protested. "Maybe he'll push Isabel out of his way, like whoever that beauty editor was who got in a brawl just to rep *Couture* on *Good Morning America*."

"It was the *Today* show," Aynsley corrected her with a smirk. "If you're going to quote the Fashionista, get it right. But either way, it doesn't matter," Aynsley explained. "If Isabel got hit by a bus tomorrow, they'd bring in someone new. Someone from *Bazaar* or *Elle* or French *Couture*. You might not know this, but Dieter does," Aynsley said, unable to keep the condescension out of her voice. How was it that out of all the interns, she—who had never even wanted this job—was the only one who had the faintest clue how the magazine and fashion industries operated?

Nadine looked miffed for half a second. "Okay, maybe not Dieter. But you gotta admit, Nelson and Wanda both seem potentially guilty. And Amelia's boyfriend works at *Style*."

"Hmm, you sure dug up a lot of dirt in a short

amount of time," Aynsley said distractedly. "Let's eat out on the patio."

"Cool."

Aynsley handed Nadine the wine and glasses and grabbed the platter and bowl of cherries. As they walked toward the patio, Aynsley saw something taped to the Sub-Zero fridge. She went to examine it: a postcard of a stone villa that read *Ciao from Umbria*.

When sent from normal parents, a postcard would probably contain a sweet little note, gushing about the sights. But Gregory and Cecilia Rothwell were not normal parents. Had they wanted to swoon about the glories of Umbria, they would've done so by shipping home a kilo of fresh pecorino, a vat of olive oil, a Renaissance painting. But no, this postcard, the fourth one Aynsley had received this summer, was a little warning, a reminder that she was being watched. The last card, for instance, had simply read: *Don't wish you were here? Get to work*. It was quite insulting, really. Aynsley had toiled eight hours a day for the last two days. She was utterly exhausted. But her parents were relentless. They expected her to put in long hours every day. She'd like to see Cecilia go three weeks without a yoga session!

She followed Nadine outside and slumped into a

chaise patio chair. Nadine was still blathering about her spy-girl mission. Aynsley zoned out, listening to the patio fountain (imported from last year's Umbrian jaunt) and trying not to think about the postcard. "Are you listening to me?" Nadine demanded.

"Yes. I'm just concentrating," Aynsley lied.

"So, you'll trail Nelson?"

"Huh?"

"See if you can't get inside his head. Maybe you should hit on him."

"I most certainly will not," Aynsley protested.

"Why not?" Nadine demanded.

Aynsley rolled her eyes. The question didn't deserve an answer. "There's no way. Why don't you, Van Buren? You hit on everyone else." Aynsley knew she was being a bitch, but she was feeling so rotten now that she had to spew on someone. And one of the great things about Nadine was that she was impervious to Aynsley's moods. Ironic, given how sensitive she was to slights from anyone else.

"Because I'm the lead investigator. I gotta keep my distance," Nadine explained.

"Plus, you don't want Sam to think you're the staff slut," Aynsley said with a grin.

Nadine laughed. "There is that. Hmm. This ham is

tasty. You're not eating? I thought you said you were starving."

Ten minutes ago, she had been, but now her appetite had vanished. She reached for her second glass of wine and made a half-hearted nibble on a piece of bread. "I'm eating," she said.

"Besides," Nadine continued, "you're not seeing anyone. You haven't been out with anyone all summer except for Walker."

Aynsley shuddered. Walker Graystone was *still* stalking her. Didn't It Boys have better things to do? "You make me sound like a spinster," Aynsley said. "Anyway, I've had some action. My Dutch treat." She was referring to Olivier, her recurring Euro-fling. Every June he traveled from Amsterdam to New York to attend some jewelry trade show in the city with his diamond-importer father, and he always made a point to see Aynsley, bearing fine chocolates, yummy hash, and his hot, chiseled body. "And don't say Walker's name. Lucy made me invite him. I can't bear the thought of seeing him."

"Speaking of, did you hear that because Callie's being honored she not only gets to go to the gala, but she also gets to bring a guest? I thought she was gonna bring your brother. You know they went on another date?"

"Please don't remind me." Aynsley groaned.

"But apparently she's not. I'm sure she's taking Ava. She hasn't asked me and she definitely ain't choosing you."

"Oh, my broken heart," Aynsley said sarcastically. Having fully determined that Callie was a fake, Aynsley was now patiently waiting, like a cheetah tracking her prey. All she had to do was watch from a distance until her moment arrived. Then, she'd pounce. In the meantime, let the little twit enjoy her time in the sun.

Nadine wrinkled her nose. "Doesn't it piss you off that Country Callie and Miss Ava get to go to the ball, and you and I don't? Shit, we *all* work at *Couture*."

Aynsley swirled the wine in her glass, focusing on *it* instead of that damn postcard. Jules had probably put it up there to taunt her. What a prick. He and Callie deserved each other. She looked up. Nadine was staring at her expectantly, as if waiting for some important piece of news.

"I mean, doesn't it bug you that we'll be left out in the cold?" Nadine asked.

"We won't be left out in the cold," Aynsley said with a smirk.

"Right, Sly. I mean, I know we'll go to some hot club

or something and have our own party, but still, it sucks that we can't go."

"Don't be ridiculous, Van Buren. Of course we'll go."

"Did you talk to Lucy? That bitch isn't gonna let me within a hundred feet of the place. She'll probably put some restraining order on me so I can't set foot in Soho Friday night."

"That bitch isn't in charge of the door. I am. You're looking at the queen of the velvet rope," Aynsley announced dramatically. "I decide who comes in, so you, Van Buren, have nothing to worry about. You're in. Jules is in. All of my friends are in. As far as I'm concerned, this is *our* party."

"You might try telling that to Callie," Nadine groaned. "The way she's strutting around, she thinks this whole shindig is being put on for her benefit."

"It's not her shindig. It's ours." As she said it, Aynsley knew it was true. Because suddenly she had that feeling, that delicious shiver of anticipation that something special was going to happen at the gala. She'd had this sense before other parties, and it always turned out to be true. The sizzle had preceded the party where she'd met Brooks Farthing, her most serious boyfriend to date, as well as the house party in Southampton that had evolved into a wild weekend in the Bahamas. And now, sitting outside on her patio with her friend Nadine, she'd had it again. Which is how she knew. Forget Country Callie. Forget Lucy, Isabel, and the lot of them. This gala was going to be a party with her people, on her turf. The glamoratti of the city would be coming out to play, and to pay homage to Aynsley—and she intended to enjoy every minute of it.

23

If the Booty Fits . . .

IT HAD TAKEN Aynsley an unusually long time to decide what to wear to Friday evening's Cutting Edge Gala. The ensemble required a certain nuance. Obviously, it had to be the three S's: stylish, sexy, stunning. Plus, it had to convey power—she was the girl in charge of the door. It also had to be a wee bit practical. Her new Roberto Cavalli beaded micromini flapper dress, fetching as it was, would snag on the clipboard she was obliged to carry. Similarly, standing around in four-inch Manolo stilettos wouldn't be much fun.

In the end, there was only one way to go. Prada.

And how handy that the Soho flagship store was conveniently located within a two-block radius of Marco's studio—where Aynsley planned to have her hair and makeup done, and do a bit of damage control (Marco was supremely pissed that Callie had canceled her appointment). And Marco's was extremely close to the Apple Store, where the main event was taking place.

Aynsley slipped out of work that Friday at four and made her way to Prada for a confab with her personal shopper. After selecting a cobalt duchesse satin Miu Miu dress with angular red cutouts, and Prada open-toe platform wedges, Aynsley skipped over to Marco's, hoping that the advance issue of *Couture* and the bottle of Cristal she was bringing would be sufficient to defang his Callie ire. Marco was less concerned about Callie's cancellation than the state of Aynsley's eyebrows, and after he shaped them, he yanked her hair into a severe chignon, dusted pale powder all over her face, and painted her lips a blood-red matte.

"Perfect!" he declared. "Dominatrix of *Couture*."

Aynsley smirked at her reflection. "Exactly the effect I was going for." After paying Marco and exchanging air-kisses, she looked at her Cartier watch, which she'd had repaired after the incident on her first day at *Couture*. It was almost six. The party started at seven, though this being New York, no one would arrive until nine, earliest. And Aynsley was famished. She checked her BlackBerry—six messages from Lucy. Screw her. Aynsley couldn't be expected to work on an empty stomach. She loped down Spring to Balthazar where she ordered a *steak frites* and a Diet Coke. An hour later, she was in front of the Apple Store, shocked and delighted to see it was already thronged with limousines and lines of partiers pushing to get inside. Not bad for seven o'clock on a July weekend evening.

"Aynsley Rothwell. Where the hell have you been?" screamed a red-faced Lucy, unsuccessfully juggling three clipboards while trying to reinsert her earpiece. "I've been emailing and calling you all day."

"I had business," Aynsley said, grabbing the clipboard Lucy was shoving her way.

"It's a mob scene!" Lucy screamed frantically.

"Wasn't that the point?" Aynsley asked, making her way to the front of the velvet rope.

Lucy pinched her face into a tight smile. "Well, yes. I'm sure we're going to be in all the tabloids. *Women's Wear Daily* has already shot a ton of film. *New York* magazine is here. A bunch of cable channels. I'll bet we even get a mention on thefashionistablog.com. We've already had Kirsten Dunst, Walker Graystone, and Tyra Banks. It's not often you get that kind of variety."

Aynsley smirked. She wasn't sure what kind of parties Lucy was used to throwing, but in her world, a mixing of luminaries was par for the course. A Mercedes limo zoomed up to the red carpet. Out popped Isabel, elegant in slate-gray Armani Privé, trailed by Nanette Lise, looking flirty in a violet Yves Saint Laurent bubble dress.

"Oh, there's Isa. I'd better go inside now," Lucy said. She handed over a headset. "Put this on. Keep it on. You need to be available at all times. Don't leave your post. I'm serious. Not even to pee."

"I'll be glued to this spot. Scout's honor," Aynsley said, before turning to wave in a group of her Dalton pals. A few minutes later, Julian arrived, looking vaguely rock-starish in skinny black Nicole Farhi trousers and a red Versace jacket.

"Nice fiesta, Sly," he said.

"Yes, quite the turnout. I didn't know if people would stay in town for this," she admitted.

Julian smiled, his lazy green eyes glinting. "Are you kidding? You've caused a reverse migration. It's like wintertime at the beach, just farmers, surfers, and yokels. Everyone who's anyone is in the city tonight."

"Isn't it fun?" Aynsley trilled. "You wouldn't believe the pleas I'm getting from the sad little people not on the list. I've been offered crazy swag: spa treatments, a Fendi bag, VIP tickets to see The Killers, just to get into this thing."

"Nice to be gatekeeper." Julian laughed. "Speaking of, have you seen Callie?"

"Can't you let me enjoy my moment?" Aynsley asked. "I don't think she's here yet."

"Well, I'd better get inside so I can greet the princess when she arrives," Julian replied.

"You do that, Romeo," Aynsley said with a sarcastic eye roll.

No sooner had Julian gone inside than Nadine slunk up to Aynsley. "Finally," she said. "I've been hiding behind that pay phone over there, waiting for you to show."

"Well, here I am."

"Is Lucy around?" Nadine asked nervously. "I don't want the bitch to see me and have a conniption."

"She's inside," Aynsley explained. "Her nose safely up the asses of several celebrities."

"Cool." Nadine relaxed. "New outfit, Sly? Looks very official."

Aynsley eyed her friend's party duds. She knew

Nadine had her own aesthetic happening, but tonight her ensemble—a leopard-print and black lace bustier and a black lace skirt so sheer that Nadine's ample derrière was on display for everyone to see—went too far. The outfit would've been risqué at the VMAs, but for a *Couture* gala, it was downright trampy.

"Sluts R Us having a sale?" Aynsley asked.

"At least I don't look like one of those Mondrian paintings."

"You're dissing Miuccia?"

"Maybe. You're just jealous because you're not as bootylicious as I am."

"So you live to remind me."

"If the booty fits—"

"Oh, go make yourself useful," Aynsley said, interrupting her, "and get me a glass of champagne and a bottle of Fiji. It's hot out here. Can't get dehydrated."

"What am I? Your servant girl?" Nadine looked insulted.

"Excuse me, but who got you in? Oh, hello, Tinsley," Aynsley said as Tinsley Mortimer sashayed down the red carpet, an explosion of flashbulbs going off in her wake.

"Hi, Sly. Fabulous party."

"Natch. I organized it," Aynsley bragged.

"I'll see you inside," Tinsley said, planting a kiss-kiss above Aynsley's ear.

"Later," Aynsley said, shooing Nadine in to get her a drink.

For the next few hours, Aynsley operated in a swirl of velvet-rope hysteria. People were acting like this was the Oscars. Everyone Aynsley had invited had shown up—her friends from Dalton, her Hamptons crew, all the visiting Europeans, a bevy of models, and the crème of the 10021 zip code. A few hundred other people Aynsley hadn't invited, but who desperately wanted in, clawed over to her, begging to make nice. Meanwhile, there was Lucy squawking into her earpiece, demanding to know whether Justin Timberlake had arrived and Sienna Miller had left. Like Aynsley knew. By ten o'clock, she'd long since given up ticking names off her list. It was impossible to keep up, what with all the hot guys chatting her up to get in and Nadine supplying her with an endless flow of champagne. She barely registered Callie's arrival out of the corner of her eye, just a blur of silver spangles and a face a little too made up to look sophisticated. Of course, Callie clearly thought she was the queen of all New York—the way she imperiously waltzed by with Ava trailing behind like her lady-in-waiting.

Ava, however, was a different story. When Aynsley saw her, she did a double take. Now *that* was a girl who knew how to pull off couture: demure yet sexy in a pale blue asymmetrical Elie Saab gown and silver Christian Louboutin peep-toe sandals, her brown hair cascading down her back in loose curls.

"Congratulations on the great turnout," Ava said as she passed.

"Congratulations yourself," Aynsley shot back.

"On what?" Ava asked her.

"On whatever you did to earn that fabulous gown and shoes. You look like you were born to wear couture."

Ava flushed with pleasure. "Thank you. Will I see you inside?"

Aynsley was about to explain that she was supposed to man the door, but then she surveyed the scene. Celebs and fashionistas were crawling all over the place, like ants at a picnic. The paparazzi were going crazy. The gawkers were, well, gawking. She'd done it. She'd helped create the event of the summer. And she'd be damned if she was going to be sidelined while Nadine, Ava, and Callie, not to mention all of her friends, got to enjoy it. Enough was enough. Aynsley was in the mood to party—and if it meant six weeks in an Umbrian prison, so be it. She beckoned Lucy's assistant over and tossed her the headset and clipboard. By the time the flustered girl could ask, "Where are you going?" Aynsley had disappeared into a throng of beautiful people.

24
The Ugly Stepsister

NADINE WONDERED HOW a party this fabulous could be such a drag. Between trying to avoid Lucy (not to mention Isabel, Kiki, and any number of staffers who were likely to throw her out on her behind), bringing Aynsley quarter-hourly doses of champagne, warding off the bitchy stares of the D&G-clad fashion zombies, and trying to get drunk on the weak wine the caterer was serving, well, this thing was about as fun as oral surgery. On second thought, that was more fun. At least when she'd had her wisdom teeth pulled, the nice doctor had given her laughing gas. It had taken her six glasses of Bordeaux to get even the slightest buzz on tonight. And what fun was it to be drunk without any-one to talk to? Sly, her usual partner in crime, was con-sumed with being the door diva.

She did a loop around the party in search of a friendly face, and counted it as a sign of her desperation that her heart leapt at the sight of Callie's mane of hair. When she got closer, she backed off. She could see that her roommate was deep in conversation with a tall guy in a sharkskin suit. Nadine did half a wave, but when Callie didn't respond, she pretended she was fixing her hair—a platinum blond wig. Seeing Callie chatting up that guy brought Julian to mind, specifically her failed attempt at telephonic seduction. What was up? Was she losing her touch? Banish the thought. She gulped a mouthful of wine and continued on, looking for a straight guy to flirt with. She slunk up the white glass stairs to Apple's Genius Bar, which currently served as the Cutting Edge Gala bar-bar. There, she spotted a gaggle of hot guys in black suits sitting on a black leather banquette. She fluffed her wig, adjusted her cleavage, and made her way over.

"Why hello there, fellas. Keeping the bench warm for a little bit of *me*?" she asked with a flourish over her skin-tight ensemble. When the guys parted, Nadine was shocked to see who they were gathered around.

Ava. Or was it Ava's über-glammed-out twin sister?

"Holy shit," Nadine exclaimed.

Ava laughed, her dimples practically dancing off her face. "Hi, Nadine," she replied, patting the seat next to her. "Isn't this the most amazing party?"

"Uh, sure," Nadine said, scooting onto the couch. What had happened to Ava? Normally, it was like she and Ava were opposites. Nadine popped wherever she went. Ava blended into the woodwork. But tonight, her dress was stunning, her hair was stunning, *she* was stunning. Not just stunning, but snap-crackle-popping.

"I think I just saw Tyra Banks. Pinch me so I'll know I'm not dreaming," Ava gushed.

"You're wide awake," Nadine replied. "And you look fantastic. That's some dress."

"Isn't it? It's Elie Saab couture."

Nadine whistled. "Pricey stuff. Your boyfriend buy it for you?" Nadine knew she was being bratty, but she couldn't help it. Ava was all Cinderella and she was stuck playing the ugly stepsister. When was it gonna be her turn to be the princess around here?

Ava swatted her with a silver clutch bag. "I told you, he's not my boyfriend. And it's not really my dress."

"Then whose is it?"

"*Couture*'s," Ava admitted. "Kiki told me I could borrow any outfit I wanted, plus shoes and accessories for the night. Then she sent me to the beauty department where they did my hair and makeup."

"Damn. Lucky girl," Nadine said, with a touch of jealousy. "Why'd Kiki go all Fairy Godmother on you?"

Ava sipped a bit of champagne and giggled. "Oh, I'm tipsy. I forgot to tell you the beginning of the story. You know how I reported on that designer last week? Well, instead of just typing up my notes, I wrote them up like I was doing a *Couture* In the Know piece. And Kiki loved it. She told me it was better than what a lot of paid staffers turn in, and she's going to run it with my byline. Can you believe it? I still can't. And she was so happy with it, as a reward, she let me loose in the fashion closet. It's like a dream. Seriously, please pinch me," Ava said, holding out her slender arm.

Well, the girl did ask. Nadine took a bit of Ava's ivory skin between her long nails and squeezed. "Oww," Ava said, jerking her wrist back and spilling champagne on her dress. "Oh, I'm such a klutz. I'd better wash this off before it sets. I'll be right back." As she disappeared toward the restrooms, Nadine couldn't help but notice how people's eyes followed Ava. It was like everyone was trying to figure out who this fabulous girl was—Nadine included.

Nadine needed a drink. Something stronger than wine. She sauntered up to the bar, tipped her chest toward the bartender, and batted her false eyelashes. "Honey, you got something for me? Red wine just won't cut it."

The bartender wrinkled his nose at her like she was a bad smell. "Oh, forget it. Just give me *that*," she said, grabbing a half-empty bottle of Merlot and a glass of champagne before stalking off. She went outside to deliver the bubbly to Sly, but the velvet rope was being manned by someone new. Great. Even Sly had deserted her. She downed the champagne and staggered back inside, weaving around all the snobby fashionistas. Screw them all. One day, it would be Nadine Van Buren they'd be celebrating.

She stumbled over a bar stool and landed right into the arms of Julian. Maybe things were looking up after all. "Hi, baby. Miss me?" she asked.

Julian's eyes flitted over Nadine's outfit to the bottle of wine in her hand. He smiled a sleazy grin. "Hello, Nadine. You're looking very rock star tonight."

"Why, thank you," she said, heaving her chest forward. "It's the hair."

"No, I think it's more the wine bottle and the drunken stagger," Julian corrected her. "Very classy," he added. "Have you seen Sly?"

"She's MIA, but Callie's over there talking to some guy," Nadine said cattily.

"She's one of the honorees," Julian replied. "All sorts of important people want to talk to her." It was then that Nadine realized that, in spite of photographic evidence to the contrary, Julian wasn't interested in her. In fact, no one at this stupid party was interested in her. Why the hell was she still here?

Suddenly, the lights, the booze, the crowds, the heat were all making Nadine dizzy. She wobbled over to a side exit for a bit of fresh air, collapsing into a chair near the makeshift patio where all the models had congregated to puff on cigarettes.

"It's smokier in here than in the bloody King's Head."

Nadine looked up and there was Sam Owens, a vision of casual suave in a sleek Hedi Slimane tuxedo jacket paired with Levi's and Prada wingtips.

"King's Head was my pub in London. East End," he explained with a sexy grin. "And I'll tell you, it was one rough lot that drank there—but these mannequins

could outsmoke them any day of the week. Models—
they can't eat food, so they breathe nicotine. Rather disgusting habit. Glad I quit." He turned to look at
Nadine, his blue eyes sparkling in the glow of the
lanterns. "You don't smoke, I hope. Bloody awful vice."

Nadine giggled. "I got plenty of vices," she said,
puckering her lips. "But not smoking. I don't believe in
anything that makes kissing taste bad, if you know
what I mean?"

"Wise girl. I knew you had a good head on your
shoulders. And a good eye in that head. In fact, I've
talked to Kiki about you. She's promised to let the
photo department give you another go."

"That's fantashtic," Nadine slurred. "But what I
want to know is when are *you* gonna give me a go?"
She stood up to rake her nails down Sam's arm, but the
ground started to spin beneath her feet. She lurched
back into her chair and looked at Sam, who was peer-
ing at her, not with the desire she'd hoped for, but an
expression of confusion and affection. Oh well, it was
better than nothing.

"It looks like you could use a glass of water. Or a cup
of coffee. Shall we go inside?"

"I'm fine. Really." Nadine stood up again, but she
felt as though she were balancing on water. She pitched

forward and would've fallen flat on her face had Sam not caught her. She buried her head into his shoulder. He smelled yummy, that baby-powder-and-sweat scent again.

"I think we'd better get you home," Sam said. "You appear to be suffering from gala overload. It's a common malady."

"Hmm," Nadine said, still breathing into his lapel.

"I've got a car waiting outside. Come on now. One foot in front of the other. That's a girl. You're doing grand." Sam took her hand and led Nadine through the party. Even in her hazy state, she could feel people watching them. For the first time that night she didn't care. Sam was holding her hand, taking her home. Maybe this evening could be salvaged after all.

Sam gently deposited Nadine into a Town Car. "Where do you live?"

Nadine gave the address and slid over to make room for Sam. "You're coming with me, right?"

Sam grinned. "I should say so. Can't have you wandering around the city alone in this state."

As the car rolled down Prince Street, Nadine noticed Sam was still holding her hand. With his other, he was opening a bottle of Evian. "Take a drink of this," he said.

"I'd rather take a drink of you," Nadine said, heaving herself into Sam's lap and sucking on his ear.

"I don't think that's such a wise idea," Sam said, gently easing Nadine off of him.

"Come on, Sam, I know you want me," she said, reaching for him again. At that moment, the car slammed on its brakes to avoid hitting a group of drunk partiers tottering across the street. Nadine's stomach lurched, and before she had time to move away, the entire contents of her stomach came up—all over Sam.

"Oh my god, I'm so sorry," she whimpered.

"Never mind," Sam said as he wiped Nadine's mouth with a handkerchief.

"But I got it all over your tux."

"Good thing it isn't a rental," he said calmly.

"I see black spots," Nadine moaned.

"Hang in there," he comforted her. "You're almost home."

The car pulled up in front of the dorm. Sam grabbed hold of Nadine and helped her out of the backseat. Nadine stumbled, barely able to walk. She just wanted to curl up right there on the sidewalk. Her legs started to buckle. The next thing she knew, Sam had scooped her up. He carried her into the lobby, up the elevator, and into her room, where he set her down on the bed. Then he pulled off her shoes and tucked her under the covers. Before she passed out into oblivion, Nadine thought she felt him kiss her on the forehead, but she couldn't be sure.

25
Everything to Lose

CALLIE HAD BEEN so worried about Isabel's reaction to her Alexandra Foxwood gown, but in the end, it hadn't been Callie's dress that Isabel cared about at all. When *Couture*'s editor in chief glided up to Callie and Ava at the gala, she grazed their cheeks with double air kisses.

"*Chères*, you look *très jolie*," she said. She turned to the handsome man in a slate-gray suit standing next to her. "This is John Conrad. He owns us, or at least Conrad Media owns *Couture*," she said with a laugh. "This is Callie Ryan. One of our interns and an honoree this evening."

"Congratulations," the media mogul said to Callie,

kissing her on the hand.

"And this is Ava Barton," Isabel continued. "Another of our interns, who Kiki tells me is a real up-and-comer. And looking so chic. *Mon dieu.* That dress looks better on you than the model who wore it in the magazine, Ava. The fashion closet is a nice luxury, no?"

"It's amazing," Ava replied. "I was paralyzed by the choices. It was too much."

"You chose well. Now, *chèries*," Isabel trilled, "go enjoy the party."

As Isabel and John Conrad walked away, Callie felt a tinge of relief—and annoyance. She was glad that Isabel hadn't thrown a fit at her unfortunate designer choice, but she couldn't help but feel like Ava was stealing some of her thunder.

She'd been shocked to see her friend's transformation. After she'd had her own hair blown out at Jean Louis David and her makeup done at Saks, she'd gone back to the dorm to get dressed and pick up Ava. When Callie had knocked on Ava's door, for a split second she'd thought she had the wrong room. Ava had smiled shyly and spun around in a little circle.

"Do you like it? It's from the fashion closet," Ava had said.

"It's gorgeous. But you didn't—"

"Of course not," Ava had interrupted. "I swore I would never do that again. Kiki told me I could borrow whatever I wanted." Ava had then told Callie all about her day, the article byline, Kiki's benevolence.

Callie knew she should feel happy for her friend. After all, hadn't she been saying all these weeks that Ava was a beautiful swan who only needed a boost of confidence? Hadn't she been cheerleading for her friend's string of editorial successes at *Couture*? It should've been perfect. The two of them were the shining stars tonight, leaving Aynsley and Nadine in the dust. Still, it would've been nice for Isabel to at least notice Callie's outfit, considering she'd put herself into hock to pay for it.

It was hard to stay jealous, however, watching Ava at the party. More fetching than her perfect dress, her $600 shoes, or her silver Tabitha clutch purse was the look on her face. She was glowing like a little kid on Christmas morning. And it wasn't like Callie was being overlooked. As soon as they said good-bye to Isabel and grabbed glasses of champagne, Lucy pounced on them.

"No playing the wallflower for you," she told Callie, grabbing her by the elbow. "CNN wants to talk to you. So does Tyra, who might want you for her show. And E! wants to film a Trend Spy segment with you. Plus,

Isaac Mizrahi says he's dying to meet the *Couture* wunderkind."

"Look at you." Ava beamed. "You're a superstar." Callie looked at her friend's expression—it was pure delight. She felt like a heel for being jealous.

"She will be when I'm done with her," Lucy exclaimed. "But you two can't be conjoined twins all night. Ava, no offense, but shoo. Callie, I want you to stand under your bio. I'm asking all the designers to pose under their blow-ups, give the industry a chance to put a face to a design."

"Okay," Callie said, and waved at Ava as Lucy led her away. Standing under her big picture, she nervously read what Aynsley had written. She half-expected a hatchet job, but the interview was pretty straightforward—sans the fact that it focused a little too heavily on her phony prep-school pedigree. Whatever. People in fashion were all about invention, weren't they?

She stood at her perch, watching the party swell. Every time a major celebrity walked in, you could smell the electric charge in the air, just like you could smell the onset of a summer storm. So far, she'd seen J.Lo and Marc Anthony, Tinsley Mortimer, and Sienna Miller, who'd stopped to admire Callie's bag and even say congratulations.

"Who's that sexy chick in the picture?" Callie looked away from her bio to see Julian, who looked wickedly adorable in a red punky jacket. He held out a rose. "Do you think I might have a shot with her?" Julian asked coyly.

Callie took the rose and smelled its sweet fragrance. "That's a secret."

Julian smiled and kissed Callie on the neck, sending a jolt of excitement down to the tips of her toes. "I'll get it out of you. I have my ways," he murmured.

Callie licked her lips. She had the urge to jump Julian right here. But once again, she couldn't. Something was always getting in the way. Kiki's call had dragged her away from him at the park. Then, on their date last week, he'd had to leave the pub early to meet some out-of-town friends. When was she going to get him alone?

"Nice turnout," Julian said, with a nod to Callie. "You and my sister did a good job."

"She definitely knows a lot of people. Did you see her at the door?" Callie asked. She had purposely ignored Aynsley on the way in. She didn't want one of her snobby remarks blowing this perfect night.

"My sister, the Prada-clad bouncer." Julian laughed. "Want to hit the bar?"

Callie shrugged coyly. "I can't. I have to stay near my bio for a while, but you can keep me company."

"Sorry, babe. I gotta work the room."

"And avoid ex-girlfriends. Nanette Lise is here," Callie said knowingly.

Julian grinned. "She's not the only one. I'll catch you later, pretty girl."

Callie watched Julian flit away, disappointed that he'd chosen to work the room instead of working on her. Then Lucy whizzed by, admonishing Callie to stay put for E! and asking if she'd seen Aynsley, who'd apparently ditched her post at the door. Callie had spotted Nadine skulking around the place, but she hadn't seen Aynsley since she'd come inside.

"Well if you see that little brat, you tell her to find me. Her ass is on the line. But that's not your problem. You just keep doing what you're doing. Everyone is so impressed with you. Here, drink a toast to yourself," she said, handing a flute of champagne to Callie. Callie raised the glass to herself and felt a delicious shiver of satisfaction. She really *had* made it.

"Cheers," said a voice. Callie looked up to see a tall guy in a sharkskin suit holding up a Sam Adams. She smiled at him and clinked her glass with his bottle. He looked vaguely familiar. Probably someone she'd seen on TV. He leaned over and began to read her bio.

"So you're Callie Ryan?" he asked.

"The one and only." Callie grinned. "Are you from E!?"

"No. You designed this bag?" he said, pointing to the picture.

"I sure did."

"Silk screen's a dying art."

"Well, maybe I can help bring it back." As soon as she said the words, she felt a change in the air and a pit of dread in her stomach. She looked at the guy again, remembering where she'd seen him before. He wasn't a reporter at all.

"I'm Quinn McGrath," he said with a tight smile. "I design hats. And I do silk screens. In fact, I did a whole series of celebrity screens that I sold to some sweet kid a few weeks ago. Turns out that sweet kid is a thief."

Callie felt the whole world crashing around her. What an idiot she'd been.

"Did you think I wouldn't find out that my design was in *Couture*? Did you think you could just take all the credit?" He asked her.

"It wasn't like that!" Callie cried.

"What was it like, then?" Quinn asked.

"I don't know. I'm so sorry. I didn't mean for it to

happen like this," Callie said, the words spilling out. "I was so inspired by your silk screens, I made the bags, and I was working at *Couture* as an intern, and the editors saw the bags and assumed I'd done the silk screens, and before I knew it, they wanted to put them in the magazine. I was going to tell you about it, I swear, but then they crashed the bags into the Cutting Edge feature like two days before the issue went to press, and I just got so caught up in everything and now here we are—"

"No—here *you* are," Quinn interrupted her with a note of bitterness in his voice. "You're being honored as a hot new designer. I'm just one of the poor schmucks who had to fight to get into this party."

"Please, don't tell anyone," Callie begged him. "Not tonight. I swear I'll make it up to you. I'll tell the editors. I'll make sure you get credit, and a cut of the profits if there are any. But if I tell everyone tonight, I'll blow everything. For both of us."

Quinn eyed Callie. She had the sense that he was X-raying her, staring right into her very soul. After what felt like forever, he broke his gaze. "I'll give you a week," he said, handing Callie his business card. "If I haven't heard from you by next Friday, I'm going straight to your editors."

"I'll straighten this out," Callie promised him. She had no idea how, but she'd figure something out.

"You'd better. Because I'm serious about this," Quinn said with a blank stare. "I've got nothing to lose."

"And I have *everything* to lose," Callie said miserably. For the first time, she realized how true that was. She'd come so close to achieving her dream, but now the whole thing was on the verge of imploding.

Quinn nodded. Then he leaned forward and gave her an air-kiss, like they'd just been having a friendly chat. "Congratulations, Callie," he sneered.

26

The Stroke of Midnight

COULD A DRESS really change a person? Ava stared at her reflection. She knew that the girl looking back was her, except—it was a different her. Maybe it was the makeup: the dusting of bronzer that gave her a sun-kissed look, the black liquid eyeliner that turned her eyes smoldering and sexy, the sheer Mac lip gloss that gave her mouth a full pout. But even before she'd been prettified by the beauty department, she'd felt the change. It had come over her the minute she tried on the shimmery blue dress that fit as though it had been made just for her. She thought of what Aynsley had told her when she'd arrived at the gala: *You look like you were born to wear couture.*

Ava dabbed at the champagne spot on her dress. It was barely visible, and Kiki had told her not to worry about mussing the garment. "Have fun. If you stain it, we have the best dry cleaner in the city," she'd said. Ava didn't want to send the dress to the dry cleaner. In fact, she didn't want to take it off. Ever. She'd never felt so good in her life, and she didn't want this night to end. Though she knew it was kind of silly, part of her was dreading twelve o'clock. What if, at the stroke of midnight, all her good fortune vanished?

"Don't be ridiculous," she told herself.

"Who's being ridiculous?" asked a voice from behind the first stall door. The door swung open and out popped Marceline, looking very forties-diva in a fuchsia Dior peplum suit and matching mile-high platform sandals.

Ava blushed. "Me. For talking to myself."

"You can get away with all kinds of *ridiculous* when you look *marvelous.*" Marceline pulled out a Chanel compact and began reapplying her lipstick. "And you *do* look marvelous. Everyone's talking about you. And about your article. Kiki's swooning like you're the second coming. Enjoy your pet status. I once occupied that glorious position."

"You did?" Ava asked. "What happened?"

Marceline snapped her compact shut and looked straight at Ava. "I'm the accessories editor of *Couture* magazine, that's what happened. So play your cards right."

Ava followed Marceline out of the bathroom and, for the fiftieth time that night, she stopped to savor it all. When she'd taken this internship last spring, she'd never in a million years thought that she, Ava Barton, the invisible girl, would be at the party of the summer. And she wasn't just hiding in a corner or taking people's coats—she was someone people wanted to talk to.

"Excuse me, but can I buy you a drink?"

Ava snapped out of her reverie at the sight of a handsome blond guy in a pinstriped suit. For a second, she thought it was Reese. In fact, she'd been seeing Reese look-alikes all over town. It was ironic that she kept conjuring up his clones when the real Reese had been emailing her funny little notes at *Couture* a few times a week since they met. So far, she hadn't replied to any of his invitations to join him for drinks or a movie. Callie would kill her if she found out, but Ava couldn't bring herself to call him. She had so many complications in her life right now—and a guy like Reese deserved a girl who didn't have any skeletons in her closet. Ava couldn't help but laugh remembering that Nadine had called her skeleton a Silver Fox. She couldn't deny it—he *was* gorgeous . . . and hard to say no to.

The blond cutie was still gazing at Ava adoringly. "So, what would you like?" he asked her, motioning toward the bartender.

"You want to buy me a drink at an open bar?" Ava asked with a smile.

The guy shrugged helplessly. "I want to get to know you a little and that was what popped into my mind. Nerves, I guess. I'm Tom Everly," he said, offering Ava his hand. "I work at *GQ*."

"Hi, Tom. I'm Ava Barton. And I have to get back to my friends. Maybe another time."

Suddenly feeling like the kind of woman who didn't need a blond cutie or a Silver Fox, Ava waltzed back to the couch where Nadine had found her earlier in the night. *Poor Nadine,* Ava thought. She just couldn't catch a break at *Couture.* Hopefully someone would figure out what a talent they had in their midst. After all, if the *Couture* editors had managed to rescue Ava Barton from a heap of mediocrity, then surely they would eventually acknowledge Nadine's skills.

"Ava? *Ava* . . ." Over the din she could hear the nasal

twang of Lucy Gelson's New York accent. Lucy ran up to her. "There you are. At least I've found one of you interns. Have you seen Callie or Aynsley?"

"No, just Nadine," Ava told her.

Lucy's face shriveled in distaste. "That little minx got in. Damn that Aynsley. Well, Nadine's the least of my problems."

"What's going on? Can I help out?"

"No. You're a guest tonight," Lucy said graciously. "But Aynsley's deserted her post at the door. Apparently she's somewhere inside partying with her brother and friends—though I can't find her anywhere. I'll tell you one thing, that girl will be lucky to have a job when I'm done with her. And Callie's disappeared, too."

"She has?" Ava asked with surprise. "But I thought she was standing under her bio."

"Me, too. And then I came over with the E! camera crew and she'd vanished." Lucy looked disgusted.

"I'm sure she's just mingling," Ava said. Though, truth be told, if Julian was in the house, she guessed her friend had run off to be with him. Cool as she liked to play it, Callie was obviously falling for the guy—*hard*. "I'll look for her and send her your way," Ava promised.

Lucy clucked her tongue. "Too late. The E! people interviewed some downtown diva with a new shop in Nolita instead. Callie's loss. Oh, look, there's R.J. R.J., darling, get over here."

A short bald man in a Gucci tux sauntered over and gave Lucy a kiss. "Ava, this is R.J. Jackson. He's a buyer for Barneys. R.J., this is Ava Barton, one of *Couture*'s star interns."

"Interns dress well these days," R.J. said.

"It's not mine—" Ava began.

"It's Elie Saab," Lucy interrupted, giving Ava a look. Ava smiled.

"It's fabulous," R.J. said. He peered at Ava for a second. "Have we met?"

"I—I don't think so," Ava said—although R.J. *did* look a little familiar.

He stared at her. And all Ava could do was hope that he didn't *really* know her. "Are you sure?" he scratched his chin. "You look a little like—"

"Obviously you've got the wrong girl," Lucy interrupted, clearly tired of any chitchat that didn't focus entirely on her. "Ava, why don't you go mingle," she suggested. "If you see Callie, tell her to find me. And if you see Aynsley, tell her she's up shit's creek."

Taking Lucy's advice, Ava climbed the glass stairs,

lit by a neon replica of the *Couture* logo, in search of Nadine. The guys Ava had been talking to earlier were on the couch, but Nadine had vanished. Ava walked to the edge of the mezzanine and looked out over the sea of people. With the enormous crowd, the swirling lights, and the flashbulbs going off, it was difficult to see anyone. Except for Julian Rothwell. His red Versace jacket made him a relatively easy target. Ava spotted him down near the entrance talking to Nanette Lise. Julian would probably know where Callie was. And Aynsley, too. Ava wanted to warn them both that Lucy was gunning for them.

As Ava made her way down the staircase, she could tell people were watching her. For the first time she truly understood what it meant to actually feel a room full of eyes gazing at her alone. As she approached Julian, the front door swung open to a burst of camera flashes. Ava put her hands in front of her eyes to block the glare and when her vision had cleared, Julian was gone—and *he* was there, looking very much like the Silver Fox Nadine had christened him. Her heart skipped about seven beats at the sight of him. Why hadn't he told her he'd be here?

"Well, well, aren't you a vision?" he said. "You're like an entirely different person."

"Thank you." Ava tried to smile. "You look pretty handsome yourself."

"One good thing about gray hair, it makes you look distinguished in a tux," he said, flirting with the full force of his charm. "Champagne?" he offered.

"No thanks," Ava said, doing her best to resist him. "We shouldn't be seen talking to each other," Ava murmured. "It's risky."

"I like to take risks," he said playfully. His smile was genuine and mischievous all at the same time.

"Well, I don't," Ava replied. And it was as if, in that moment, she had finally summoned the strength to do what needed to be done. "I've been thinking about our situation," she continued. "I don't think I can keep doing this anymore," she said abruptly.

His brow furrowed. "Sweetheart, you don't mean that—"

"It's over," Ava said, cutting him off. And with that, she walked away, exhaling months of pent-up fear and guilt. Deep down, she'd wanted to do this since the summer began. But she'd been paralyzed by the little voice in her head that told her she couldn't do any better. Then, tonight, it was like the dress had made her superhumanly confident. As she turned and walked away, she felt bold, strong, and free. She *could* do better.

She could do whatever she wanted.

Ava scanned the room, taking in all the fashionistas who tonight, even if they hadn't meant to, had embraced her as one of their own. Off in the distance, she spotted Julian's red jacket and, next to him, Callie's tawny mane. She grabbed two glasses of champagne from a passing waiter, but just as she was about to make her way over to her friend, she heard the old-fashioned chiming of a nearby clock, made louder by the open entryway. Ava searched the room for a timepiece, finally seeing that it was midnight. She listened for all twelve gongs. Then, when the last one had struck and a new day had dawned, she looked down at her dress, her shoes, her bag—all of her magical props were still with her, along with a tingling new sense of excitement and confidence. Ava's Elie Saab dress would soon go back in the *Couture* fashion closet, but the new Ava wasn't going anywhere.

"All I can rectify is that the party's just begun." —Nelly Furtado, "Party"

Filed under: Fashionista > Style

One of the biggest perks of being the Fashionista is having an all-access pass to <u>runway shows</u>, boutique openings, and the ultimate luxe treat: fashion-magazine parties. It's a tough job, but somebody's got to do it.

Recently, the Fashionista attended the red-carpet ride known to insiders as the <u>*Couture* Cutting Edge Gala</u>—and oh, what a ride it was! Some girls enjoy caviar and champagne, others might choose a spa day at <u>Bliss</u> or a luscious chocolate dessert—but the Fashionista would trade all of the above to party at the *Couture* gala once more.

It was an event complete with plenty of celebrity »

skin—A-listers decked out in <u>Marchesa</u> gowns, <u>Cartier</u> jewels, and strappy <u>Louboutins</u>. But the downtown boho chic girls were out in full force, too—many of them pairing frilly <u>Alexander McQueen</u> skirts with shimmery <u>Alice Roi</u> camis. And, not to be outdone, the uptown elite were in attendance as well—decked out in <u>Chanel</u> and <u>Valentino</u>, of course. Then there were the fashion luminaries: like *Couture*'s <u>Isabel Dupre</u>, who looked glamorous in that *oh-so-French* way of hers, a vision in <u>Armani Privé</u>.

But the Fashionista's favorites are the wild cards—the Cinderellas of the ball whom no one who's anyone had ever seen before. One filly in particular really took the Fashionista's breath away: a willowy beauty in <u>Elie Saab</u> who looked like she'd stepped out of a dream. *Who was she?* you might ask. Well, she wasn't a Hollywood star or a supermodel or a socialite of a scandal-sheet regular. Actually, she was a "lowly" *Couture* intern who outshone all the designers and fashion dominatrixes the party was meant to honor.

Ah, *quelle surprise*! That's one of the Fashionista's favorite things about this crazy fashion business: watching caterpillars turn into butterflies.

Until next time,

Your faithful Fashionista

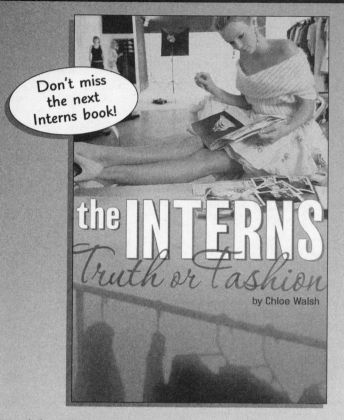

Welcome to Wellington: Just because you're rich, brilliant, and perfect in every way doesn't mean you can survive boarding school.

Check out the first three novels in the Upper Class series!

The Upper Class

No one ever thinks they'll crash and burn in their first semester—but someone always does.

Laine is a born Wellington girl: rich, sophisticated, blond. Nikki is everything a Wellington girl shouldn't be: outlandish, sexy, from a new money family. Laine and Nikki couldn't have less in common. But to survive first semester, they may have to stick together—or risk being the first girl to go down in flames.

Miss Educated

Just because you survived first semester doesn't mean you can relax.

Chase is this close to being expelled from the prestigious Wellington Academy. Parker, on the other hand, is doing just fine academically—it's her social life that's on probation. When a campus tragedy and a little fate bring Chase and Parker together, Wellington finally starts to make sense to them both. If only it wasn't so easy to mess everything up.

Off Campus

A new year at Wellington means new students, new drama, and the same old rule: Don't get caught.

Nikki is an old pro at the boarding school thing now. She's ready to show someone else the ropes, someone like Delia. A transfer student with a dark past, Delia doesn't quite fit in anywhere, but she sure knows how to have fun. But when fun leads to sneaking off campus, it can very quickly turn dangerous.

HARPER TEEN
An Imprint of HarperCollins*Publishers*

www.harperteen.com

A fabulous must-read!

ALMOST FABULOUS

MICHELLE RADFORD

Now that her former-rock-star mom has finally stopped moving their family around, fourteen-year-old Fiona Blount only wants two things in life: Predictable Routines and Total Anonymity. But then she discovers that she has the power of mind control. And she finds out that her mom might be getting the band back together for a big concert. And she learns that her long-lost father might not be so lost anymore. Suddenly, Predictable Routines and Total Anonymity seem more out of reach than ever.

What ever happened to a girl just getting up and going to school and being normal?

HARPER TEEN
An Imprint of HarperCollins Publishers

www.harperteen.com

What happens when best friends become worst enemies?

The first in a series!

Best friends Avalon and Halley could rule their San Diego middle school—if they could only stop fighting with each other. Soon these two besties become full-blown worsties. From returning clothes borrowed long ago to drawing up a list of who gets which friends, Avalon and Halley are about to learn just how hard it is to battle the one person who knows you best...and isn't afraid to use those secrets to get what she wants.